The Night I Knocked on His Door

Layla Marden

Contents

Chapter 1

LUCY

My parents always had their alarm clock set on six in the morning. That way they could get ready for work and I could get dressed for school. The routine worked well - I never once had a conduct mark for being tardy to class and for an elementary kid that meant everything, almost as much as having the most colors. That was until I came into the third grade and the chaos began.

It was three in the morning on a Tuesday and my parents woke up to loud crashes from the kitchen. My dad instantly grabbed the house phone and dialed nine-one-one while my mom was the one to speck out the situation. She had dad's hockey stick up in the air, ready to knock the intruder out cold if she had to. The authorities by then were heading out to our house while my dad made his way to my room to get me.

"You better get out. . . I have a gun!" My mom made the sound effect of her taking a safety off. That wasn't the first time she had been through a robbery and she picked up on tricks to scare them away. She even had a security system installed but it wasn't blaring off, so she figured the intruder must have came through a window or something.

There was more clashing of metal from around the corner which made my mom's grip tighten on the hockey stick. She had prayed every night for her not to defend her family this way, but it looked like my mom had no choice. It was either the trespasser or our family.

Sucking in a breath, my mom built up enough courage to peek into the kitchen. In the dark she could barely even make out the cabinets and island yet alone a shadowing figure.

Another crash made her jump back, flinching into my dad. She turned around, ready to pull back and wait for the authorities with him, but my dad had a different agenda.

He strode into the kitchen and dared to flick the light on. My mom was horrified up until she followed behind him and found the little intruder.

Low and behold it was me in my Barbie night gown.

"Lucy! What in the world are you doing?" My mom dropped the hockey stick with shaky hands and grabbed onto me.

She had expected a hug back but when she received nothing, my mom spun me around. She was met by two vacant eyes, a mouth muttering incoherent words, and a beautiful stream of drool dribbling down my chin. For some reason in that state of attractiveness it made my parents scared even more than the thought of a burglar breaking in.

Or at least that was what they told me the hundreds of times they retold the tale. Apparently ever since I began to sleepwalk I suddenly turned into the walking dead and could never hold the memory of it for too long. Because they never stopped retelling it. Never.

"Guys, seriously. Don't worry about me tonight around my friends. No locks, nightly checks - oh, and definitely no motion detectors. Please no motion detectors. That would be bad considering the fact Cara has the bladder of a peanut." I wrapped up the last of the party favors, eyeing my parents. When I received disgruntled expressions I sighed. "Okay, you can do the nightly checks. Seriously, though. Be quiet. Wouldn't want to wake them up or something. What - why are you looking at me like that?"

"Why do we need a reason to look at you?" My dad hid his smile well. "You're our beautiful seventeen year old girl, after all."

"That reminds me," I pressed my lips in a thin line, "-- do not say stuff like that tonight. Weird, weird, weird. Did I mention weird?"

Thankfully my parents let my anxiety churn without their help, exiting out of the kitchen while chuckling among themselves. They never understood boundaries - even with each other - and that tended to leave me in awkward situations. Whether that be because they made out when ever they felt like it - horrifying sight - or the sudden outbursts of affection they wanted to bestow upon me in public. I never enjoyed being touched and yet - despite them knowing this - they did it anyway. I would get a big, sloppy kiss on the cheek whenever a friend from school walked by us in the mall. Or a huge hug that took me off the ground and landed me feet away from my launch point.

The ding of the oven took the image of my parents kissing out of my head. Thank the lord. I padded around the kitchen island and put on the oven mitts. The scent of strawberries poured out of the oven once I opened it, a perfect pink cake made with love catching my eye.

"Damn it," I hissed lowly. I told my dad multiple times to buy a new pair of oven mitts and he always answered with a definite yes. Two weeks later and I was burning myself on my birthday. Typical. "Fuck."

The pan was dropped onto the counter before the heat became unbearable. I half expected my parents to reappear due to the oh-so-familiar sound of crashing metal, but they did not. Thankfully the cake remained in tact too, but I could not have said the same about the oven mitts though. With one last hateful glare, I threw them in the trash. Then, observing my hands, I refrained from yelling out at my dad what a liar he was. He really needed to back up his words.

Before I had a chance to begin the buttercream icing my phone buzzed in my back pocket. I quickly took it out, the I.D. Little Chicken flashing. It was funny, really, how friendship worked out. You could call each other the craziest of things yet it doesn't phase each other. According to the dazzling Jacklyn Kate Jensen, I was her late-night-booty-call-without-the-booty. Some might be offended by such a reference, but I adored it just as much as I adored her.

'Can I come early today? Parents are being -' Her choice of emoji made me laugh. It seemed her parents were resembling a pile of shit. I wasn't surprised, though. Jacklyn Kate's parents were insane. They were very adamant on choosing every step J.K. took her whole life. And since graduation next school year was nearing they wanted to talk about college nearly twenty-four-seven.

I was quick to answer. 'Of course. You can help me with my cake!'
'Okie dokie, sounds fun.' J.K. replied.
By the time J.K. got to my house I was already done with the cake. It was two hours later, only thirty minutes before my party began,

when Jacklyn Kate trudged in and dropped her bag of stuff on the floor. When she saw I had finished the cake, she frowned.

"I told my parents you would do it without me," she mumbled. "I could have made it look like a million bucks, but no, I had to talk to colleges on the phone."

I gasped. "What are you saying, my cake looks bad because I decorated it?"

J.K. wasn't afraid to hurt my feelings. "Basically."

"Shush, shush. That isn't what you're supposed to tell the birthday girl." I swatted her away when she tried to grab me in for one of her infamous hugs.

She only smiled then tried again, that time succeeding. "Happy Birthday, Lucy!"

"Thank you, J.K.." I chuckled, then squeezed her. "Can you believe how old we are getting?"

"I know right?" She dared to dip her finger into the side of the cake - my cake - and lick the icing off the end. "We're almost adults. That is freaking scary."

The thought was mind boggling and very, very scary. Was I even ready to go off on my own? I've barely even started driving, yet alone bought a house and get a job!" At this I blew out a heavy breath, shaking my head. "Don't even remind me." I nearly shivered.

Eventually time flew by and I found my house full of hungry, loud teenager girls staring at my cake with big eyes. It was very flattering, but I was determined to wait until later in the night to eat it. So, I cleared my throat, catching the attention of all my close friends.

There was Cara Inane - the one who was drinking my bottles of root beer. She had just come back from soccer practice and she was tired of drinking water and Gatorade at her house. Her dad was strict on her diet, and soda was a definite no-no. So every time she came to my house she drowned herself is sodas, no matter the type. Even the cherry flavors, despite the fact she hated them. So there she was, the jock in a grass stained soccer uniform, her fifth soda protectively in her hand.

"Do you have any Dr. Pepper, Lucy?" she asked while sipping the last of her drink.

Abby was the one to answer for me. "She doesn't." At that Cara frowned, throwing the empty can in the trash. When she turned away Abby leaned in towards me, a smirk on her face. "Do you have any Dr. Pepper?"

I laughed. "Yes, I do. Back of the fridge."

Red hair whipped at my face - that was how fast Abby took off to the fridge. She was always a bundle of laughter, and that moment was no different. We met barely a year ago in art class but it was friendship at first joke. She was corny, hilarious, yet extremely serious when it came to her favorite things. Exactly why she was seriously grabbing a Dr. Pepper out of the refrigerator while keeping an eye on Cara's back. She must have wanted all of them to herself. Typical Abby.

The last VIP at my party was the one and only Jacklyn Kate - who felt it was about time for cake because she took the liberty of grabbing my parents from canoodling in their room to sing Happy Birthday.

"Everyone, come around the counter, please. Time to sing our hearts out," my dad said, grinning wide. ".. Or we could just eat the cake." I struck him a look. "Okay, yeah, I guess we gotta sing."

All too soon the sound of dying animals sounded through the air, scaring my cat Rachel out of the room. Even so I could not wipe the smile off my face. I was surrounded by people I cared about and had a delicious strawberry cake in front of me. Who wouldn't be happy?

"Alright sweetie, make a wish." My mom pressed her hand on my back.

I paused for a few moments, taking this wish very seriously. Ever since my sixth birthday when my wish actually came true I had taken the time to think. So I did just that: thought. I could have wished for prosperity and health, but I took a much more selfish approach. I wanted a certain someone to finally notice me. He didn't need to ask me out or become close with me. All I wanted was for said guy to realize I existed and remember my name. That wasn't hard, was it?

And so I blew out my candles wishing just that.

After my friends devoured half of the cake and played some Wii games with my family and I, we eventually settled inside of my room. I had planned to spend the rest of the night without my parents, but apparently they didn't realize that. Again, they never thought about boundaries.

What was next, we would braid each other's hair and gossip?

So I wrinkled my nose, stopping them from entering my room with a bowl of popcorn. "What are you dong?"

They each gazed back at each other before looking at me. "Going to watch the movie.." My mom finally answered. This earned them a frown. "Oh, okay." She finally realized. "A movie in our room."

My dad still had confusion written all over him but he just followed my mom. Once they wrapped around the corner and disappeared from sight I shut my door.

"Okay, now that my parents are gone," a wicked smile crossed my face, "who wants to watch something on Netflix like the crazy young kids we are?" When I received an applause, I bobbed my head. "See, this is why we are friends." I clicked my tongue. "We completely get each other!"

Everyone laughed. Everyone except J.K. who was looking too awestruck at her phone.

I grabbed the nearest thing by me, Cara's socks, and then chunked them at J.K.'s direction. At first she did not even react, but when she did, those fiery green eyes I knew so well seemed to bore into my soul. "Excuse me," she choked on her words, throwing the soccer socks back at me. "Can't a girl stare at Clayton Hugh's new Instagram picture for just a second? I didn't know it was a crime to stare at something you would never even get to touch."

"Clayton?" Now I was the one choking, making all eyes turn towards me. Was I really that obvious? "I highly doubt the picture deserves to be stared at for more than a few seconds. Lemme see." At this J.K. wiggled her brows at me. I could attempt to downplay Clayton Hugh, but there was no use. J.K. could see right through me. "Wow, okay. What kind of guy takes a selfie of himself shirtless when he is supposed to be mowing the lawn?"

"Obviously Clayton." Cara grabbed the phone and eyed the shirtless boy in the image. I wanted to snatch it back. Stare at it more. See if I could zoom in and catch those blue-green eyes in a moment of heat. But I refrained. That in itself deserved a pat on the back later on. "He is so hot." Cara sighed. "Why can't all boys look like him?"

"I don't get the appeal that much," Abby chimed in from her corner. She already had out the candy from the party favor, ready to watch a movie. Clayton Hugh was just another distraction to her. To be fair though she was never a fan of the baseball player. Once she called him a meat-head jock with no flavor. Abby wanted someone spicy. Unique. Not so perfect, I supposed. "Now can we please watch the movie." She huffed, busy unwrapping a Twix bar. "Please."

To be honest I did really want to watch a movie but talking about boys felt like we were in a movie ourselves. It was weird to think, I knew that, but it felt like we were in one of those chicklit's at a slumber party. We would talk about boys, possibly play truth and dare, then one of us would be dared to venture out in the late hours seeking said boys' hearts. It was far from reality, but it was cool to think up. Especially if the guy would be Clayton.

Clayton Hugh was a total heartthrob in every sense of the word. With his tussled blonde hair and exuberant smile, he was exceptionally good looking, a great pitcher and first basemen, charming, smart, and even had the room to fit in being artistic, too, if everything else wasn't enough. That wasn't even mentioning the fact he was foreign, with a cute little Norwegian accent. He had moved here permanently three years ago after doing time in the exchange student program at our school. That was when it started. The very thing that lead me to use my seventeenth birthday wish on him.

"Okay, c'mon now. We gotta hold off on him since he is all Lucy's." J.K. patted my knee with a wink. "She is basically in love with him after all."

"In love?!" I choked for what felt like the hundredth time that night. "Dude, no. I am not anywhere close in love with him," I exasperated. When J.K. raised a brow I sighed. "I mean, I am definitely interested in him - not in that way. More like, uh - like a crush or something. I don't know. Yeah."

Which was completely true. At the time being I had a school girl crush on Clayton. It was sweet and innocent. I didn't desire his body like a lot of other girls had. All I wanted was to talk to him, get to know more about his life in Norway, possibly go on a date. Then again what girl at my school - besides Abby - didn't like the sound of that.

"When you guys have babies together one day--" J.K. looked straight at me, fire in her eyes, "-- i'm going to say I told you so."

Scoffing, I shook my head then grabbed the T.V. remote from her. Jacklyn Kate was so insufferable at times. Dealing with her it looked like I should have just left the cliche movie scenes inside of the movies.

It was nearing four in the morning and after four movies and a whole cake my friends were fast asleep. They looked so sound snugged in their sleeping bags. It almost made me want to fall asleep too. Almost. Instead I continued scrolling through Netflix trying to find another movie to watch, my eyes bloodshot and beginning to become itchy.

When I suggested having a sleepover for my seventeenth birthday my parents warned me something like that would happen. My anxiety would keep me on edge and awake all night. And if I finally were to fall asleep my sleepwalking would be restless - possibly dangerous to myself and the people around me.

I should have listened to them, but a flash of hope for a normal life had caused me to blindside my logic.

The sound of my door clicking open barely even caught my attention. It wasn't until my dad whispered my name a few times before I noticed his presence. It must have been four by now because my parents did hourly checks on me, switching every hour shift.

"You need to sleep, Lucy." He sighed when I shook my head indignantly. "So are you just going to stay up all night? That's what you are gonna do?"

I nodded. I was too exhausted to do anymore.

"What if you slept in Jacob's room?" That hung thick in the air for a long time. Most of it I was trying to process what he had just asked. "We'll be able to lock you in there. Motion detectors if you want them." He too mimicked my actions and yawned. "Just c'mon, already. Before your friends wake up."

Slowly my blurred vision casted over the sleeping bodies in the room. They looked so peaceful. I wanted to look that peaceful when I slept.

I scratched at my eyes. "Okay," I mumbled.

Eventually I found my way to my brother's old room. There was a few times I almost toppled over and fell asleep right there in the hallway, but thankfully my dad was alert even when he was exhausted too.

"Almost there." My dad guided me around Jacob's boxes of things and to the bed. "There you go," he coo'ed like I was a child. "Now you can sleep."

I nestled under the sheets, enjoying the leftover scent from my brother. He had been gone for nearly two years now and his smell had never left. It was so comforting. After giving me a kiss on the cheek and setting the motion detector down on the ground, my dad eventually left, not forgetting to lock the door.

I laid there for what felt like ages. Eyes closed. Breathing steady. Heart calmly thumping in my chest. I felt so at ease with the world; that nothing bad could ever happen if I just slipped into a slumber and fell into a wash of peace.

Maybe tonight would be the night my sleepwalking would end. Just maybe.

A ghost of a smile played its way on my face at the thought. Then I fell asleep.

Chapter 2

C LAYTON

Thump, thump, thump.

The loud knocks echoed throughout the house making my eyes shoot awake. At first I thought I was imagining the whole thing, but after another set, I was certain. Squinting over at my alarm clock I winced when I made out five in the morning. Either those annoying Girl Scouts - that did pack a mighty hit - were starting business in the early hours or someone was trying to break through the front door.

"Mor, far (mother, father)! The freaking door!" I yelled out for my parents while attempting to rub the sleep out of my eyes. After a minute passed and I received no answer I put my glasses on. "Of course I would have to be the one to get it." I muttered. "Selvfølgelig (of course)."

Against all my wishes I sat up straight, fixing my glasses to sit on the bridge of my nose. Fatigue passed through me; the thought of curling back in bed and ignoring the rather adamant person at the door sounding better and better. Even so I made my way out the door, a frown plastered on my face. At least it wasn't a school day, I attempted to reason. Now that would have made me angry.

All of a sudden when I entered the living room the pounding stopped. Had they gone away? There was a tiny bit of hope in me, but it only got crushed when it started back up again. What teases.

I blinked a few times before pressing my eye to the peephole.

"Nå tuller du med meg (You must be kidding me)." I mumbled.

The pests were not Girl Scouts this time around. Instead they were two of my past close friends Zeke Sams and Mateo Raeken. I preferred the scouts more than them.

"What the hell guys?" I whispered, anger laced between my words the best they could without drawing the attention of my parents. If they knew these two were here they would send them packing. "It is five in the morning!"

"I am sorry, I didn't know I missed an episode of no shit Sherlock." Zeke rolled his blue eyes. His hair was relaxed, falling over his forehead as if he woke up like that. "But c'mon, we are going to play some right now. Bring an extra pair of clothes though because we're gonna hang after."

My English wasn't the best, but I knew every word he said. Yet I kept waiting for a question. The question asking me if I could even venture out at such a time. "Um, okay." I eventually answered their impatient gazes, that question never coming up. "One second."

Before the guys ended up barging into my house and demanding me to move faster I swiftly put clean clothes in my baseball bag, threw on sweats, then replaced my glasses for contacts. If I had taken a few seconds longer they would have stepped inside but when they saw me coming they stayed put.

"I'm gonna go in my car," I told them. "You guys head out so I can write a note for my parents."

Zeke breathed in, catching himself before he said something he shouldn't. He was a very organized person, and I guessed us driving in different vehicles wasn't apart of his original plan. He might have said extremely impulsive things, but his actions definitely weren't. So when he took India Logan to Homecoming and ended up sleeping with her, that wasn't a surprise to him - which was exactly why he had reserved a hotel room for that night. If she wasn't interested though, he wouldn't have forced her into anything, but he would have became disoriented. Upset. Confused, even.

Mateo, on the other hand, was far more simple to pin down. With Zeke's matching blue eyes and brown, typically styled hair; he was a follower.

"Alright," Zeke eventually said. He ran a hand through his hair. "See you there." I watched as the two hopped back in Zeke's car. "Better not slack in getting there like you do with running the bases!" Zeke yelled as he rolled down all of his windows so his loud music could be shared with the entire world.

I smiled in return. If I had said something it would have been in Norwegian and not very kind.

After the sleek ride pulled out of my driveway and zoomed out of sight I rushed back into the house. My instincts were telling me to wake up my parents and tell them I was going out, but instead I resorted to the note idea. I scribbled down I was heading out with my teammates to practice then hang out. I had no clue when we would come back but I felt like twelve was a good estimate time. Not too early, not too late.

But Zeke apparently had other plans.

Most of the day consisted of working out and baseball, but once we called it quits after eight hours out on the field Zeke insisted we go and walk the mall strip after hitting the showers. Before I would have taken that as an opportunity to buy something, but I knew these boys good enough to know that the only reason to go was to see the opposite gender shopping.

"Hey, doesn't that girl go to our school?" Zeke's question lead all of our gazes wandering around the music shop. There were a good amount of people inside, but none I recognized from school. "The girl right there, the one with the head phones on. She is kinda cute, yeah?" When neither Mateo and I spotted the girl Zeke huffed. He pointed her out. "That one."

My eyes focused in on the girl. She had turned her back towards us before I could catch a glimpse of her face, so I was quick to ask, "What's her name?"

Zeke snapped his fingers. "Ah, I got this." More snaps. "I think it starts with an 'L.'"

I found my lips puckering out. The mystery was enticing.

"I'll go see." The boys whistled at me, drawing the attention of nearly everyone in the shop besides the girl. She must have been enjoying what ever song she was listening to because her head was starting to sway back and forth. "Hold kjeft (shut it)." When I received blank expressions I just rolled my eyes and chuckled. "Be back in a few."

Sometimes Zeke and Mateo made no sense to me. I never said I was going to ask her out or anything. All I wanted to do was go and see who she was, possibly put a name to the face. Maybe that was the difference between the American boys and I. Not everything involving a girl included flirting to me - though if I was interested in this one, then possibly. Possibly.

The old records felt smooth under my touch as I slowly waltzed over to the blonde's ail. I watched with a faint smile as she picked out Enslaved's album. That was one of my favorite rock bands and they just so happened to originate from Norway. I had no idea anyone from the states listened to them; especially such a petite girl. The thought of seeing her rock out to their songs stretched my lips even further.

"Great band," I commented while grabbing a capsule of record cleaner. My thumbs fiddled with it as I waited for a response, but when she didn't even glance my way I realized she had not heard me. The boys were already laughing at my failed attempt behind me. "Great band," I repeated once more, this time much louder.

The girl visibly shook, the album falling out of her grip. Wide green eyes caught me off guard as our gazes connected. Even when clear recognition passed through her face she still looked frozen; frightened to the point of no movement. Under her gaze I felt like a scary monster, not a guy she would ever be interested in.

It was a shame, too, because Zeke had hit the nail on the head. This girl was most definitely cute. I had always thought that since we had chemistry class together. Her hair was wavy and messy yet it looked put together in a way. Unlike during school she was wearing a dress; one that forced me to give her a glance up and down. It was sweet, a perfect match to her shy nature. When I met those doe eyes and noticed she stiffened even more I instantly regretted my actions. Zeke and Mateo were becoming bad influences on me.

Before I crashed and burned I willed myself to send her a slight smile before turning on my heels and bolting back to my friends. Evidently to them I had crashed and burn.

"So she does go to our school?" Zeke asked, still chuckling. They lead me out the door so I could recover.

I rubbed at my forehead. My face felt hot at the touch. "Yeah... It was Lucy. Lucy Walker."

"Well, well, well. Look at you knowing her name by heart." Mateo poked my cheek. "She is pretty hot though, so I don't blame you." My nose wrinkled at this. "What? I can't think she is attractive?"

Of course he could have thought that, but applying the term hot to a girl was not cutting it for me. It didn't taste right on the tongue. "Well, yeah." I ran my hands through my hair. "But she would never go for guys like us."

Zeke almost toppled over laughing then and there. "She would never go for us?" He sounded more disgusted than amused. "Sure she isn't ugly but she isn't anywhere near out of our league. If anything it is the other way around!"

The two laughed with each other while I held a serious expression. There wasn't anything funny to laugh at - well, other than the fact how pathetic they were. I could have laughed for hours thinking about how indestructible they thought they were.

Finally though, enough was enough. "Alright, alright. Come on guys, let's go back to your place." I cleared my throat, maneuvering around the conversation of Lucy. Zeke had no right belittling her into a corner, even if she was out of sight and ear shot. She deserved respect. "Shut up about Lucy and move it."

My far once told me something before I went into the exchange program. It was about romance. He told me it wasn't the flesh, but the heart that you fell in love with. He even backed up his theory by using the example of him and mor.

"How else could she have fell in love with me?" He would joke.

And while Lucy Walker definitely wasn't picture perfect, I was positive behind her shyness there laid a great human being. Yet Zeke was here laughing his rumpe (butt) off, acting as if she was some sort of beast.

"Wow, someone is testy." I could feel one of them trying to cave in the back of my knee to make me trip as I walked towards my car. "Does our little Norwegian have a crush or something?" The two snickered. "How adorable."

"Hvorfor er jeg venner med dere to (Why am I friends with you two)?" My whole face scrunched up. Oh, yeah - because they introduced me to my life: baseball. "Glem det (forget it)."

Silence followed and for a split second I thought they actually understood what I had said, but instead they were only taken for the woman walking across the street. She was battling to keep her dress skirt down and unlike me, they never once turned away. It was foolish of me to think Zeke or Mateo - yet alone both of them - actually backed up their words about learning the Norwegian language for the sake of their friend.

"Dude, can you stop speaking that gibberish?" Once the two landed back down to Earth Zeke sneered. "It sounds annoying."

Oh how many times I thought that back when I first met them. My far had always taught me the English language growing up, but not enough to be fluent. Yet I became an avid English speaker when I wanted to become closer friends with Zeke and Mateo. All I wanted was to connect with them more, but I couldn't say the same about them. That was the exact reason why I stopped reaching out to them unless they were the ones to approach me.

"Actually, I have to home right about now. Parents just texted me," I lied, my teeth grinding.

"Okay, see ya, bud." Mateo pushed at my shoulder hard while Zeke eyed me before waving me off. He wanted to intervene, I could tell. He most likely had going back to his place as a part of his plan.

But when we dispersed in different directions I couldn't help but let out a relieved breath.

I should have listened to my instincts.

"A note does not suffice when you are going to be gone the whole day, Clayton!" My far was livid when I entered the house at seven. He wore that face that clearly meant you-should-know-better-than-that. "You should know better than that!"

All I did was groan. Maybe if they had woken up when I kept calling them to answer the door my day would have been spent differently. "Well it wasn't like I was having a blast." I breathed out. "Plus Zeke and Mateo sort of dragged me out of the house," I said. Far did not look convinced one bit. "I am fine. Tired, though. They woke me up at five."

Thankfully far wasn't the parent to dig any deeper for information. Mor, on the other hand, would have questioned me on everything we did. That was mildly annoying, but the worst part was that she could tell when I was lying. I had a clear tell and yet I couldn't manage to change it. I had hoped old habits would die hard someday.

"Night," I said, grabbing a box of cereal from the counter for dinner.

Far still looked bothered by my nonchalant attitude. ".... Night."

That was why I loved mor working so late. I would have been in that kitchen for another hour or so being interrogated.

I took a mouthful of Fruit Loops and kicked my way into my room. I dropped my baseball bag on the ground, tore off my shirt and jeans, then leaped onto my bed. It was so welcoming. So friendly. That was the least I could have said about Mateo and Zeke, although they did have their occasional friend moments. Like when we played baseball for instance; our love for the game was like a glue that kept us together. Even if we were to fight when we went out on that field and threw back and forth it was like we were back in the ninth grade.

Putting more cereal into my mouth I took a glance at my night-stand, the joyous flavor on my tongue not enough to keep me from frowning. There sat my phone in its broken glory. The same phone Zeke and Mateo thought it would be funny to throw like a baseball to each other. Of course since Mateo wasn't the best catcher he missed and it went plummeting to the ground. Mor and far were infuriated when I brought it back to them. So much that they cut off my phone from their plan and said if I wanted another I would have to get a job and buy one myself.

Sometimes I regretted it all: going into the exchange program, persuading my parents into moving to the states, and most impor-tantly leaving Norway. It was such a nice place - or I thought that at least, but I could have been biased since that was where I was raised.

I could tell my mor missed Norway too. A few times I walked in on her looking through old photos she took of the beautiful country. Even so when I questioned her she insisted she was happy. And I could tell she meant it.

"Missing one thing doesn't mean I am not happy with what I have now." She blessed me with those words often.

It had been almost four years of living in Ridgewood yet in that moment I was questioning whether or not I was truly happy. At the beginning it was great. I had the friends I thought I could count on, the attention of girls, and a sport I was decent at. But as the years went by the friends changed. Or maybe I changed. Those girls were still giving me their undivided attention, but I was not interested anymore. There were very few that peeked my interest, but most of the time they never even approached me. The only constant in my life there was baseball, and without it I probably would have moved back to Norway in a heartbeat.

And so as I laid there, preparing to sleep off the rough day, I tried to focus in on the positives. My parents were with me and extremely proud of the life I have created here - well, when I wasn't getting in trouble because of Mateo and Zeke. School was work but I managed well enough. Many colleges were interested in me playing ball for them. So it wasn't all bad.

I sighed into my pillow, then soon enough fell asleep.

Chapter 3

LUCY

"Wait, hold on one second! What happened?"

I proceeded to jump up and down as I gripped onto J.K.'s hands. The moment after the music store fiasco with the Clayton Hugh, I basically dragged Jacklyn Kate out of her dance class. She was the one to drive me to the mall strip, and the original plan was for me to shop until she was finished with practice, but everything changed the moment Clayton approached me, spoke to me, and smiled at me. Then there was the fact he basically ran away from me, but I could throw that over my shoulder.

My whole face was elated. "Clayton Hugh happened!" There was a lot more jumping. "He came up to me in The Tunes!" More jumping. I could feel the eyes on me but I did not care. "He even smiled at me, J.K. And oh my gosh it was beautiful. Gorgeous. Stunning."

Jacklyn Kate processed my story then soon enough she was bouncing up and down with me. "Seriously?" She gasped for both air and words. "What did you do?"

What a good question. It was such a good question that my feet fell back to the ground and off cloud nine when I realized I did nothing. Absolutely nothing. I was one hundred percent positive I stood there like a deer in the head lights. No wonder Clayton ran off! I scared him off.

My smile gradually died down, along with J.K.'s happy jumping, so I covered my face in my hands. "Oh, God." I groaned. "I am such a loser." I felt the vile coming up my throat.

Leave it up to Lucy Walker to scare off her crush. Who else would besides me?

J.K. attempted to move my hands, all the while questioning me what was wrong, but I insisted in staying in that position. I wanted to hide from the world - more importantly, hide from Clayton Hugh the rest of my life. That was impossible though. I had to show my face at school on Monday and he would be there two desks in front of me in chemistry class.

"I froze, J.K. Froze!" I began to pace on the corner of the street. Jacklyn Kate was not the best person at calming me down. If anyone was it was Abby. J.K. was trying her best though, so I gave her the benefit of the doubt.

J.K. was beginning to get overwhelmed. "Dude, calm down." She shushed me, no doubt peering around us and taking notice of the people staring. "I'm sure you didn't freeze that bad!"

I snorted into laughter. If I remembered clearly, then I did. Badly.

When I made that birthday wish I should have mentioned the subtle addition of me not embarrassing myself when I finally got the chance to talk to him. Then again fate would have taken that and twisted it too somehow.

"Ugh." I sighed, seating myself on the window sill of the nearest store. My head was beginning to spin. This was all too much for one day. For one crush-struck girl. "Sorry, Jacklyn Kate..." I glanced over at her with a small apologetic smile once I breathed.

Her face was still contorted with confusion. "I sort of want to know everything that happened exactly, but I'm--I'm afraid you would freak out again." She confessed with a smirk. "But hey, the love of your life smiled at you, yeah? He probably thought you were a babe." Her right eye dropped into a wink. "He would be stupid not to."

I pushed at her shoulder lightly. "First off, he is not the love of my life!" When she gave me a jaded expression I only shook my head more, yet my smile remained. "And yeah right, like Clayton would think that when he has Courtney literally throwing herself at him."

Courtney Fisher was his on and off again girlfriend. Or at least that was what she gushed about in class. It was funny when you were shy. Most of the time it was a negative. But when it came to sitting around some of the most popular girls in school they assumed I never listened in on their conversations. How could I not though? They surrounded me! I was right in the middle of their juicy talks, so of course I knew a lot more than I should have. Not to mention their definition of whispering meant talking at an average level.

"That fish? Whatever, she blows, and he knows that. Why else would he have came up to you?" She patted where I had hurt her, before adding, "And I like this version of you. Very unpredictable. So emotional. I dig that."

I gawked at her. "J.K. are you hitting on me?" My eye lashes fluttered. "It is about time! I've been lusting over you for years."

We laughed among ourselves, clutching each other's hands. It was times like those that made me feel the happiest. Jacklyn Kate was my best friend, and I could not stand the thought of us dividing after high school. Her parents were dead set on colleges out of state, while I was going to stay home due to my sleeping condition. Sure there were video chats but it wouldn't have been the same.

I would still want my best friend at my side, ready for whatever sarcasm she had to say next.

"Time to take you home so we can tell your parents we're eloping!" J.K. grinned down at me as she stood up. "I am so ready for the honeymoon."

Oh how I would miss Jacklyn Kate Jensen.

The rest of the day was just as emotional as before, but only in a different setting. J.K. and I had been locked up in my room for hours talking, laughing, and occasionally getting into heated fights. Yet like any other time we parted on a good note: with a handsy hug and wink. My parents laughed at us and bid J.K. farewell before shutting the door and turning towards me with a look of disapproval.

"What?" I asked, rolling my eyes. I knew they were upset about me bringing J.K. here without their permission, but they were the ones telling me to be social. That would mean inviting people to my house, not just for my birthday.

Their expressions confirmed my thoughts. "All you had to do is give us a heads up or something. Maybe I could have cleaned the house up for company."

"J.K. doesn't care if your part of the house is dirty. My room is clean and that is where we go!" I bit down onto the sandwich I put together, gazing at them pointedly. "Not my fault you guys dirty up a clean house so fast." Pushing past them, I placed my plate down on the kitchen counter and opened the fridge to get the missing ingredient: mustard.

"And did I hear correctly that you talked to a boy today?" My mom came to my side, her attempt at being quiet a failure. That instantly caught the attention of my dad, and soon it was yet another family gathering only in the kitchen.

His face was priceless. "A boy?"

"You were snooping again?!" I sighed, shutting the refrigerator door harder than normal. "This is another reason for me not to invite people over. You guys can't mind your own business."

These two were absolute pests when it came to my social life. When ever I brought friends over they coincidentally had to do laundry at the same time. That way they got to listen in on us. Yet the majority of the time my parents put out on washing clothes because they were lazy.

"Uh, um. Excuse me young lady, but you are our business. Now who is this boy and should I go get mom's shotgun?" My dad placed his hands on his hips trying to look intimidating. Clayton Hugh towered over him, and the mere thought painted my cheeks. "Are you thinking about him right now? No, no, no. You are forbidden."

I cackled alongside my mom. "Forbid-dden?" I was starting to hiccup as I laughed.

For the most part my parents were cool - too cool, so to have heard my dad so frazzled about a boy who I never had a chance at was amusing. He stood there with a frown, his hands firmly glued to his hips. He reminded me of a much, much tinier version of Wreck it Ralph.

"I'm going to go and open up the presents I got in the mail today. .." I shook my head, chuckling. "You don't have to worry about any boys, daddy. Boyfriends are overrated. I don't want or need one."

It took a while, but eventually his expression softened. "Oh okay. Okay- um, good. Good."

I was glad he believed that, because I sure didn't.

I still could not believe the birthday present my Aunt May decided to get me.

It was was bed wear, but not exactly for sleeping. The short-shorts made me cringe as I tried them on, reminding me very much of my volleyball spandex when I used to play. They were tight in all the wrong places, had the accent of lace on the sides, then sported PINK in big letters on the butt. At least they told me where to return them to.

If the bottoms weren't bad enough, the top was just as risky. It stopped just below my bellybutton, enough to show off a good two inches of skin, and had a deep v-neck that displayed what little cleavage I had to offer.

This was meant for the opposite sex. Not for me to sleep comfortable in.

I honestly had no idea what she was thinking when buying this.

"What is wrong with it?" My mom asked, eyeing me up and down. I felt so exposed. "It looks cute to me!"

I gawked at her. "This is like. . . not for sleeping, mom." My attempts at sugarcoating never got through to my mom. "This is for girls with boyfriends, or something." Another blank stare. Then finally I huffed. "I have no one to impress, making sweats a great option right about now."

My mom tsked. "You have it all wrong, Lucy." She stepped inside of the room and towards me and my mirror. When she stopped behind me, and looked at her daughter through the mirror, her smile was light and airy. "No woman wears something like this to impress anyone besides themselves."

It took me a for moments to digest this, and when I had, the corner of my lips quirked up. Barely. After forgetting how uncomfortable I was, my eyes scanned my body, and I found my mom's words to be true. When the bottoms weren't riding up, and my top was placed in the perfect spot, I was impressed. Impressed but very, very uncomfortable. How could anyone wear stuff like that every night?

So I hurried my mom out, exclaiming I wanted to head to bed. I didn't want her to call Aunt May and tell her I was changing out of her present, so that was the best I could do without drawing anymore attention to myself. She argued at first, saying we could hop in to bed together and watch movies, but eventually she got the message I wanted to be left alone.

Once the door clicked shut I stepped back in front of the mirror, scanning over myself one last time.

The girls used to always tease me then that I slept like a little girl in my pajamas. They would sleep in stuff like that - short-shorts with a tank top. I assumed they did it for their boyfriends, but whenever they rode the single train with me, they would not change their attire.

So why couldn't I indulge myself with something different like they do?

Not wishing to think one more second over it, I crawled into my bed. It was cold at first, but once my body adjusted, sleep fell onto me quicker than ever before.

Chapter 4

CLAYTON

My sleeping pattern was effected greatly by Mateo and Zeke's visit the day previous. So much I had fallen asleep at the early time of eight then woke up, fully rested, when the sun was still down and would remain so for a while. I knew Zeke was an early bird, but I never pictured five in the morning to be a perfect time to throw around.

Nonetheless the two were the reason why I was roaming the kitchen around four, my stomach growling for breakfast. I knew my mom had a busy day so I decided it was best to stick with a bowl of cereal, even if the idea of eggs and bacon sounded delicious.

So as I stuffed my mouth with Fruit Loops, my mind wandered away from my ex friends the best it could. I noted that I had still had to finish my English report on the U.S. economy. Then there was that baseball bat I ordered online that should have been coming in any day then. Last but not least, the date I was tricked into with Courtney Fisher was later that afternoon.

It was a long, long story on how that happened, but I wasn't as stoked about it like all my baseball teammates were. Sure Courtney was extremely appealing to the eye, but life wasn't all about that. I only had one class with her, which was chemistry, and her personality was definitely a huge turn off - actually, she reminded me a lot of Zeke. They both spread lies, gossiped way too much, and enjoyed attention from anyone and everyone.

Sadly I fell in that anyone and everyone category.

Don't get me wrong, it was sweet for Courtney to have had a crush on me, but I thought I made myself clear the twenty other times she asked me out that I wasn't interested. I guess one could have said her determination was an admirable trait in her. A trait another guy would truly appreciate, along with everything else that came with her. It was just I wasn't that guy for her.

Right when my mind is off the topic of Mateo and Zeke, the two could not help themselves but become the center of attention once again.

There was knocking at the front door.

It made me curse out and crunch the little Fruit Loops in my mouth harder with agitation.

"Guys, seriously, I don't feel like going out today --" I swung the door open, my breath hitching in my throat.

It was not Zeke. Or Mateo.

Instead there stood a girl; a girl who was extremely under-dressed to be wandering outside of her house. Her hair was a mess, a lot of it covering up her facial features, and when I listened in closely and blocked out the crickets, I could hear her mumbling stuff faintly.

"Are you okay?" I instinctively took a step outside, eyeing the area before gazing back at her. There was a bad feeling sinking into my stomach. When there was no answer in return, that only made my worry grow. "Can you tell me where you came from?" My hand reached out slowly, cautiously. I wanted to see if she would retract, scared to be touched. "Come inside, I can help.. We can call who ever you need." Her skin was cold at the touch. Goosebumps were up and down her arms.

By then panic was beginning to set in me. This girl had obviously been through some unimaginable scenario. She could have been abused; scared to the point of not speaking up for herself. Or possibly raped.

A shiver ran down my spine.

"Watch your step.. watch your step." I had to pick her up into the house, my words not registering to her. "Mor, far! Wake up!" I yelled out. "Help!"

I placed an arm around the girl's waist, guiding her more efficiently to my room. I would have placed her in the living room, but that was under construction for remodeling. She fell onto the cushion of my bed without hesitation, laying down and curling into a fetal position. She was beginning to shiver, so quickly I turned the ceiling fan off and placed a wool blanket over her. Then, making sure she was comfortable, I ran to my parents room.

They were both shuffling in their beds, barely even awake. I wanted to scream at them, saying there was a possible victimized girl in my room, but instead I used my energy dragging them out of bed. Far was absolutely furious with me, demanding to know what was going on, while mor was busy dodging furniture. However when I pushed them into my room and pointed out the girl with shaky hands, they fell silent.

"Why is there a girl in your bed?" Far asked, eerily too calm.

My mouth was open to speak, but fear was over taking me. I don't think I was ever more scared in my entire life.

"S-she was at the...the front door." I eventually said, eyes staring at them wildly. "I don't know what is wrong with her... but something is wrong."

That was all it took for mor's instincts to kick in. Sleep was tossed over her shoulder and she speed towards the girl, ordering far to call nine-one-one and for me to help her with an inspection. My breathing was beginning to become erratic, so I had to calm myself the best I could. After rubbing at my face and steadying my breaths, I stood opposite of mor, watching as she began to move the hair out of the girl's face.

Immediately upon that I stepped back, sure that I was going to be sick.

"That is Lucy.. Lucy Walker." I covered my face, cursing into them.

Who the hell would do that to someone as sweet as Lucy?

"Yes, a girl came up to our front door and.. and.." Far entered the room with the phone, looking to me for an explanation. "My son opened the door, so here he is. He can tell you everything."

"Ye-es, um." I pressed the phone to my ear but it wouldn't keep still. "Lucy Walker came up to our front door. She was, uh, disorient-ted. Could barely even walk."

"Sir, I need you to calm down for me. Can you repeat the name of the female?" The dispatcher asked.

I couldn't tear away from Lucy's closed lids.

"Sir?" The woman repeated.

"Lucy-y," I sputtered. "Lucy Walker."

There was a long pause, the sound of her typing killing me as every second went by. Mor had removed the blanket and began inspecting her limbs for wounds.

"We are sending an ambulance and squad car over there imme-diately."

And she meant it. Within minutes the authorities came.

They removed my family out of my room while a paramedic tended to Lucy so they could question us. It felt like hours we were sitting there around the dining table, explaining our parts in tonight's situation. For a second I thought they had everything they needed, but then two people stormed into the house. They were dressed in their pajamas exactly like my family, and their eyes were wild with emotion.

"Lucy is this way, Mr. and Mrs. Walker. She is safe and healthy." A cop assured them.

The Walkers never gave my family a glance. They followed after the cop in a rush.

Eventually everyone else left the table, leaving me to suffer in my head. I wished there was something I could have done.

"Are you Clayton?" A voice shook me from my dozing off state. It was Mr. Walker, the man who stormed in not too long away. He didn't seem as worried as before. If anything he was relieved, which made me feel less tense.

I nodded, gulping.

"I'm Andrew Walker, Lucy's father." He sat down beside me, mak-ing the dining room feel less empty. My parents went to introduce themselves to the Walkers leaving me to dwell in my worry. "Lucy and her friends have mentioned your name once or twice before."

My brows rose. Why would Lucy and her friends mention me? I never figured I was in the same atmosphere as them. I was simply another jock who had the jock friends and the cheerleader "girlfriend". Too one note for them.

"They have?"

He nodded. "Yep. You must be a hit with the ladies."

The amount of nonchalance in his voice is extremely unnerving. "Not to be rude, sir, but why are you telling me this when your daughter is in trouble?"

Mr. Walker instantly shook his head, eyes becoming far more serious. "She isn't in any trouble, son."

A weight lifted off my shoulders. "She isn't?"

"No, no. It is a miracle she is fine, though. Walking across the whole neighborhood could have had an ugly turn for the worst."

Walking? A simple walk around the neighborhood doesn't explain her still being in her pajamas, the inability to speak, and appearing so disoriented.

"I don't understand..." I admitted sheepishly.

Lucy's father cracked a weak grin. "Lucy has this condition called somnambulism." He repeated. "You may know it as sleepwalking."

Sleepwalking? My brows quenched together. I had heard of it, of course, but I never knew anyone that actually walked in their sleep. Yet alone managed to get out of their house and walk across a whole neighborhood. It was a miracle in itself that she never got seriously hurt. She could have been hit by a car!

Shifting between the floor and Lucy's father, I was speechless. That was a bizarre experience I never wanted to go through again. I thought the absolute worst had happened to her.

"She does this every night. Sleepwalk. But tonight was different since she managed to get out of her room. The house." Frustration made its way on his face. "I don't know what more we can do.. We have tried so much." He rubbed his face.

The paramedic that inspected Lucy further came back inside the room, putting his phone back in his pocket. He said he called Lucy's therapists and doctors, who said there was no need for hospitalization unless she had an injury. Luckily enough Lucy had none, so after filing report and signing papers, the chaos of authorities left, leaving my family with Lucy's.

The sun was beginning to raise, a stream of light illuminating the small frame in my bed. My parents offered to help move Lucy so the Walkers could take her home if they wanted, but everyone agreed it would be best if she slept there until she woke up. She had already been tossed and turned enough for a night.

"Why don't you go wash up, son. She will be fine alone for a bit." Lucy's father came back into the room, smelling of bacon from the breakfast mor prepared for everyone.

I wasn't sure to take that with offense or respect, since he was basically saying I looked like a mess, but then again I couldn't blame him. When I looked into the mirror and saw my appearance, it was cringe worthy. My eyes had dark circles clinging underneath them, and my eyes were bloodshot.

A shower was exactly what I needed to gain enough energy to get through the day. When I stepped out I felt rejuvenated. It was finally setting in that Lucy was going to be fine, so there was no need to worry anymore. After slipping into the clean clothes I set out for myself, I cursed when I realized I never brought in a shirt.

Wanting to be as quick as possible, I swung open the bathroom door and went back towards my room in a haste. I figured Lucy would be asleep so I wouldn't have to feel self conscious.

But when I came into my room and saw Lucy standing, peering at a framed photo of my family, I was voided of embarrassment.

"Lucy?!" I couldn't hide my excitement.

She jumped up, mimicking her reaction from the music store yesterday. Only this time her eyes were dead set on my naked chest.

My emotions were getting the best of me though, because without thinking clearly I went over and grabbed her into a hug. I was so happy she was okay. Awake.

"Thank God you are okay." I whispered into her hair, squeezing her tight.

I didn't even mind that she never returned my gesture.

All that mattered was the fact she was awake, healthy, and safe right in that moment.

Chapter 5

LUCY

My whole body was numb. I had felt like that ever since the moment I woke up that morning. From waking up in a room that wasn't mine, realizing I had slept in Clayton Hugh's bed, to the hug we shared, and all the way up to meeting his family. Heck we were driving away from his house and to my own and I was still numb. All I felt was a tingling sensation everywhere.

"We are going to have dinner with the Hughs tonight, Lucy." My dad broke the tense silence.

I was so lost inside my own head that I didn't hear him. He had to repeat it louder to get a reaction out of me. "What?"

No, no, no. That could not happen. I never wanted Clayton to see my face again. I already had the idea of switching out of chemistry class to a different one to avoid him entirely.

"No, daddy." I whined. "Please no. No. Just no. I can't."

"Why not? All of us are extremely happy you are okay, and we wanted to celebrate that. Plus the Hughs are a very nice family." My mom chimed in.

Were they really that oblivious? Could they not see the pain written all over my face? No - they had to have. At least mom had to have, I went to her last eye appointment and her eyes were perfect.

Or maybe it was me. If I pulled the corner of my lips a tad touch lower, deepening my frown, and stopped blinking back my water works, they would have seen the fear. Humiliation. Heartbreak.

If it were any other house - even the President's - there would have been one less emotion running through my body. The heart-break was not caused firsthand by Clayton at all, but with him in mind, and every other wild thought, I was self destructing.

"Please, no. I'm, um," I quickly thought of something, "tired. Really tired."

There was a silence, and by the focused look on his face through the rear view mirror, I could tell he was thinking.

"Then that's good! You can walk yourself to the Hughs again for dinner!"

I groaned, bumping my head into the back of my mom's seat, in turn making her groan as well. Despite that, my eyes remained on my feet-- my sock covered feet. The last time I wore socks were ages before - maybe as far as a month previous. So the only logical reason where those socks came from was from the same owner of the gym shorts and t-shirt I was wearing.

Humiliation passed through me for the hundredth time, cursing my leap of faith last night with wearing Aunt May's revealing present. But when I thought about it, wearing Dumbo printed pajamas wouldn't have been any less embarrassing. That would have been worse.

"Someone shoot me and put me out of my misery."

My brother Jacob was always a very calm person. He was tidy, or-ganized, and the epitome of a perfectionist. So whenever I wanted to clear my head or distract myself from the world, I went through some old planners of his. A few were from his high school years, one from his freshman year in college, then the most important one of all.

It was camouflage, funnily enough.

He didn't mean much when buying that particular planner. Jacob only thought it was a cool pattern. I would have known because I was there with him strolling through a Dollar Tree.

12-7-13

Go see Lucy at her cross country meet at Hindenburg High School.

I remember the seventh of December that very year. It was the day I won first place - the last time I played a sport in school. Running was something I had always done since I was small, but unlike my parents, I hated it. I didn't want to spend my mornings outside jogging, yet alone in the heat of the afternoon racing against other girls over a course of four miles.

So after my last meet, I had planned on going out to a big dinner with my whole family, since Jacob was driving in from college.

12-8-13

Talk to the family about the decision.

The decision.

The thought made me close the planner shut to admire the beauty of the metal stars pinned on the front of it. His decision was just as beautiful as the shimmering stars on that planner; yet just as dangerous as the real ones burning up above.

Once my mind was clear enough to at least stand up from Jacob's bed, I placed the planners I read through back in the correct box, then headed back to the modern times.

The time was here. In the dark the clock of the car illuminated, taunting me every block we got closer to Clayton's house. My mom had picked out my outfit, but only because I did not have the energy to skim through my closet. It was cute nonetheless; a flushed pink color with lace decal at the skirt. When I put it on my anxiety lessened. That didn't last long though.

For the first time I had a real chance to take in Clayton's home away from home. I had known he lived in my neighborhood as of a few months back, but never did I know which street he lived on, yet alone household. Yet when my dad pulled into the cute house with the yellow window sills, I realized I had passed by his home every day. I even recognized the touch of yellow multiple of times, always thinking it was bold and interesting.

He was so close yet still managed to be far away.

"Alrightio, darlin'." My dad turned around to send a toothy grin. He was enjoying this all too much, but that was only because he thought I was trying to be funny or something. Who knew what he thought; he only figured I wasn't scared to death.

I mean facing the boy you have been holding a crush on for years isn't scary at all. Especially when you walked to his house with bed hair, drooling, and little to no clothes on. It would be a walk in the park, actually.

Oh, wait - no, it wouldn't be. Exactly why I was shaking in my flats as I moved slowly up the steps leading to the Hugh's front door. The yellow from the shingles matched the door, and while any other time I would have found it adorable, the blinding color was making me sick.

I stood there, clenching my stomach, in hopes something would go wrong and the dinner could be cancelled or rescheduled.

"Are you going to knock?" My dad nudged me.

I huffed.

"Fine then, I will."

With every knock to the door the quicker my heartbeat sped.

One, two, three, four...

Please don't throw up, please don't throw up, please don't throw up...

The inevitable did happen though, and the door opened. The very blonde I was hoping wouldn't be there held a large, welcoming smile.

It was Clayton, and he looked as handsome as ever. He was wearing a lavender button down with khaki pants, and besides the fact that shade of purple was my favorite color, I found myself having to catch my breath. He had that smile on his face; the one entirely too perfect that made my lips remain shut in shame.

"Hi, Lucy." That smile. Gosh. "Mr. and Mrs. Walker." He bobbed his head, acknowledging my parents, yet his gaze never left mine. He made my insides constrict. "Please, come in. My parents are setting the table right now."

He was so polite; everything I had ever dreamed about. When I fantasized about the moment our parents met, I had imagined it a lot like that. Other than the whole sleepwalking drama earlier that day, that is. Plus the fact he and I were no where near girlfriend and boyfriend. Also my urge to vomit wasn't in my dream either.

I gulped, my fingers clinging onto my dress skirt. "Okay."

I thanked my lucky stars that the Hugh household was chilly so my blazing cheeks could cool off. Adding red to an extremely pale girl only lead to an even more embarrassing situation.

Sure enough Clayton's parents were in the dining room: Mr. Hugh placing down utensils while Mrs. Hugh put out a bowl of what looked to be a type of stew. When they heard my family their eyes flew up, blinding me with striking shades of blues.

"Hello, Lucy!" Mrs. Hugh wasted no time to trot around the table and grab me in a hug. I have never been a fan of touching, but when you smell like Mrs. Hugh, you could grab me anytime. She smelled like sugar cookies. The kind with rainbow sprinkles. "So happy to see you again, and so soon." She laughed, prompting me to snort out a fake one. I sounded like I was dying. "Glad to see you are doing good now."

Up next was Mr. Hugh, and unlike his wife, he felt hugs were awkward. Well, with how he put it, he explained in this long speech how he was horrible at giving hugs and that a fist bump would be better suited. I understood him on a spiritual level.

After the welcomes dinner was dived into rather quickly. I made sure to seat myself down after Clayton sat just to make sure I was in the farthest chair away from him. Mrs. Hugh shortly described the menu, and the fact I was going to eat Norwegian food was taking my mind off Clayton.

"So, Lucy, how are you feeling?" Mrs. Hugh asked politely, picking at her food with a fork. She had such gorgeous blue eyes; a mirror image of Clayton's.

My stomach sank at the thought.

Keeping my eyes low and away from the boy diagonal to me, I answered, "I am doing... okay..."

Another silence fell over the table; the subtle munching on food the single disturbance. The awkward level surpassed that morning by a long shot. I had never felt so uncomfortable before. If it wasn't showing in my body language or my vague answers, I wasn't sure how else to get the message across. All I wanted was to lock myself in my room and cuddle with my hamster. I wanted to erase every memory of today and go on about my life without Clayton Hugh seeing me as that-girl-who-sleepwalked-to-his-house.

"Well I am really glad you are doing okay." The voice made me visibly shake. So much my fork tattered against the plate. All eyes flew on me.

I stared hopelessly in between my parents, desperately wanting them to understand me, but instead they held the same confused looks the Hughs were giving me.

Clayton cleared his throat so he could continue. "Can you tell me more about your sleepwalking?"

I tried so hard not to glance at him. Too hard. Yet I still failed in doing so.

Our eyes connected momentarily before I decided his plate of food was much more comforting. "Um. . . It started when I was. . ." My throat was growing dry. My insides were suffocating me. If I had known it would be that hard to talk to your crush, then I would have never made that birthday wish.

"Oh my God," I suddenly blurted out, the pieces coming together. The birthday wish.

The confusion on everyone's faces was hard to miss by then, so I quickly got up and excused myself. Mr. Hugh pointed out the powder room and I graciously headed in that direction.

I needed space. That was what I needed.

So as I entered the cramped restroom, I froze in front of the mirror, only breathing. It felt so calming to stand back and just breathe. It had to have been an hour tops since the last time I truly did so.

Once I was calmer, I repeated the words of my birthday wish in my head.

I wish for Clayton Hugh to realize I existed and remember my name.

What a little trickster Fate was. My simple wish was construed to this awful mess. If there was one thing I knew, Clayton certainly knew I existed and knew my name by heart by then. Well, my name or by a ridiculous nickname like sleepwalker girl or something.

It was like my tenth birthday all over again. I had wished for a puppy, and what did I get? I got a stuffed animal puppy that only had one eye since my brother thought it would be funny to pull off one of the buttons. I remember being so upset and throwing a tantrum, only to end up with no puppy of any kind. My parents took back the stuffed animal and threw it away because of my attitude, and thinking back on it, I wondered how fun that puppy would have been if I have it a chance.

A chance…

A small smile glossed on my lips. It was fleeting, but definitely there.

Sucking up my stomach of nerves, I took a chance and headed back to the dining room. My entrance took everyone by surprise, the small talk Clayton and I's parents created dying down for a mere moment. I managed to curve the corner of my lips upright, then sat back down with poise.

"So, um. . . I heard the baseball team is playing George Ranch next Friday. Are you ready for that tough game, Clayton?"

J.K. would be so proud of me not stuttering or tripping over my words. That deserved a Sonic milkshake, so I duly noted that while maintaining eye contact with Clayton. It was such a thrilling thing yet so small. I looked tons of people in the eye per day, but never had I gotten such a skyrocketing adrenaline feeling in my gut. A portion of it was me feeling sick to my stomach, but the thrill was there.

"Hopefully," Clayton answered me with a tentative smile.

He was a true baseball prodigy, and there he was, sitting there with a shy, humble front.

I licked my lips, my smile growing. "I ha-ave no doubt your team will win."

Despite my stutter, his own lips widened. "Thank you, Lucy. . . I appreciate that. Really - I do."

The night went from there. It was easy, breezy, and beautiful - the complete description of a Covergirl cosmetics product. Sure, I was awkward at times, but so was everyone else. I learned a lot from that sit down. Not just the fact Mrs. Hugh could cook a mean lapskaus and and swede puree, but that talking to Clayton wasn't all horrible on my end.

"It was great having you all over, officially, this time." Mr. Hugh chuckled when raising his glass of wine. The adults raised their own wine as well, while Clayton and I settled for apple cider. "May this be the unconventional start of a great friendship, yeah?"

"Mest sannsynlig," Clayton spoke in Norwegian.

I felt like a fool not knowing what he said, but by the kind expression on his face, he had to of agreed. And the idea of becoming friends with Clayton Hugh was music to my ears.

"We can only be friends if you come to my game Friday, though." He smiled cheekily.

"Sounds like a deal," I readily replied.

And to that we clinked our glasses.

Chapter 6

CLAYTON

I was not ready to pitch up against George Ranch.

My curve ball was atrocious; every time ending up in the dirt. The speed of my fastball was sub par at a whopping seventy-nine miles per hour. Even my hitting was off - I fouled more balls than actually making correct contact for a hit.

"Are you up for twenty more?" I asked far, kicking the dirt at my feet. My voice resembled my gloom, so I had to speak up. "Can you keep throwing more at me? And I need faster pitches. George Ranch won't be taking it easy on me."

The sun beat down on my face, sweat cascading down my forehead. We had been at it for nearly four hours, and if I looked sweaty, far was drenched.

"Clayton, you have practice tomorrow." He stepped off the mound and wrangled his hand out of the glove. "That was enough for today."

No. We couldn't be finished. I still had so much to improve on. Plus I needed a valid excuse to not go out with Courtney for the second time in the past couple days. Last Sunday we were supposed to go out, but I ended up backing out of that because of the Lucy Walker drama. Then I rescheduled to Tuesday, and now that the day was there, I wanted nothing else but to stay on the baseball field and keep my head in the game.

"I'll stay then. Get out the pitching machine - yeah, the machine." I rubbed the back of my neck then dried my hands on my dirt stained pants. "I'll be back around four."

I thought far was going to make me go home by the look on his face, but suddenly his expression twisted into bemusement.

"Does this have something to do with Lucy going to the game on Friday?" He asked, the humor in his eyes unmissable.

I smacked my lips then rolled my eyes. I was not about to get into that when I needed to practice and perfect my technique. "Uansett far. Vi snakkes senere (Whatever, father. I will talk to you later)."

"No, no. You are not getting rid of me that easily." Instead of heading to the parking lot he started towards the home plate and me. My eyes continued to remain on the diamond shaped base mat. "You are never nervous for a game. Especially against George Ranch. We always beat them." He had a point. I hated when he had points. "So what's different now?" He pretended to ponder, but he and I both knew the new adding factor. "Oh, yeah, it is Lucy Walker."

"What are you trying to say? I am nervous to play in front of Lucy or something? Because that is far from the case!" He looked to barely believe me. "I've seen her in the bleachers for past games. So technically nothing is different from those past times."

Which was completely true. I had seen Lucy in the bleachers multiple times this season. She and her friends would always sit in the front corner closest to the dug out when they watched. Plus it wasn't as if I noticed her first. Zeke was the one to point out Lucy's best friend - Jacklyn Kate was her name, I believed - and commented on how she was hot. In turn I took in the people surrounding J.K., and boom, there was Lucy, clapping and cheering for the run. From then on I only noticed a pattern.

It wasn't as if I were picking her out from random seats every game.

He puckered his lips, the twinkle still in his eye. "Tell me, son, how you are barely even able to find your mother and I in the crowd, yet you can find Lucy?"

Why couldn't he drop the subject of Lucy? My nerves had nothing to do with her. It was all about me and my tiring arm. It was all about me and my swing. It was all about me, and only me.

"You can think what you want, I honestly don't care." I spoke defensively with a sour expression. He was wasting my precious time. "I'm going to get the machine."

I never gave him a chance to say anymore, because I was already off.

Courtney was becoming insufferable.

I was the type of guy to give every girl a chance, and definitely not hurt someone's feelings, but it was getting to the point of me not giving a damn. I had explained to her, in whole honesty, that I wanted to focus on baseball that week. I told her. But what happened?

She showed up at the baseball field with tons of other people, making a whole spectacle. Zeke eventually popped up with tables, and the food came in with the twenty other people showing up. Football was being played in the right field, eating was off by the home plate, and then there was me, sitting on the pitchers mound, wanting nothing more than to be left alone.

The sky was clouded, mimicking my mood, and when Mateo started my way, it grew darker.

"Hey, man. Why the long face?" He held out a bottle of who knows what.

I declined the gesture with a simple shake of my head. "Oh, um. Far - my dad - just texted me saying I need to start heading home." I lied through my teeth. "I'll see you at practice tomorrow - yeah?" The smile curving my face never met my eyes. Typically Mateo wouldn't catch something like that, but when he frowned, I sighed.

"But you're feeling okay, right?" He asked, popping the lid off the bottle. It smelled like root beer, surprisingly. When I didn't respond, he moved on. Typical. "Hey I see you got a new phone..."

I chuckled halfheartedly, nodding my head. It cost me two months of chores and allowances to get enough money for a new phone; to replace the one they recklessly ruined.

"How long have you had it?" Mateo wrinkled his nose, peering down at his own phone.

What did it matter to him?

"Uh, Monday." I answered skeptically.

"And you haven't called or texted me?" The confusion was so real in his voice it was almost laughable. That was until his frown deepened, the true expression of worry crossing over him. I hadn't seen Mateo like that since freshman year when Brynley Curtis stood him up on a movie date. "Oh, you must have lost your contacts." He breathed out with his reasoning.

I had the contacts. If it were Zeke I might have even told him that, but it wasn't him.

"Yeah, that's why. ." I pretended to shuffle through my phone while he told me his number.

He smiled at me. "Well I'll let you get going. See you tomorrow, bro."

With a small wave and last sip of root beer, Mateo headed back towards the group, who was busy around the barbecue pit.

It reminded me of past times we would gather at that exact baseball field and celebrate wins, but that special feeling was gone. My special baseball field was no longer having celebrations for victories, but instead to fill the need of us teenagers.

Before I turned to leave, Zeke caught my eye over in right field.

The others guys playing with him had ran to the hamburgers and hot dogs a few minutes back, and now it was only him and another girl throwing the football back and forth. She was strangely familiar. Then when I looked closer I realized it was J.K. - Lucy's close friend. That short bob was unmissable.

Her smile was hard to miss too. She was so smiley it was blinding all the way from where I was.

"Clayton come over here and throw with us!" Zeke suddenly yelled out, waving me over. His typical smirk expression was instead replaced with a grin, resembling J.K.'s to a tee.

Although the idea of hopping in my car and leaving sounded great, I wanted to speck out what exactly was going on before my eyes. I knew good and well Zeke had his sight on J.K. since sophomore year, but never once had I seen them together. Mateo and I always asked him why he never asked her out only for him to change the subject entirely.

I held my own smirk, waltzing over. "You can leave now Zeke, J.K. has her a good throwing partner now." Zeke was the only one not to laugh, but that was not a surprise. What was a surprise was the red seeping onto his cheeks. "Hey, Jacklyn Kate." I grinned towards her and received a shy smile. "I haven't talked to you since sophomore year, huh? When we had Ms. Anderson for Geometry?"

"Oh, God, do not even get me started on that class. We were all so bad." She exasperated.

I wasted no time to nod my head in agreement. That class, as a whole, was extremely disruptive.

Zeke thought it was smart to throw the football at me mid-conversation. "I called you over to throw with us, not to socialize," he spoke with a smile being held up by pins.

I patted down my shoulder where the ball hit me. "Okay, okay. No need to get your panties in a twist."

J.K. giggled at the two of us. "It's okay, Zeke. I actually have to go right about now. My cousin should be done with his Boy Scout meeting." She pointed towards the recreational building across the park. "Thanks for inviting me to play some football while I waited for him to finish. See you at school tomorrow?"

"Oh -" there went those pins keeping his smile up "- yeah, sure. Have a good morning."

I puckered my lips out, confused. Last time I checked it was verging into the night.

"Evening, I mean. Evening. Yeah, evening. Um. Yeah." He took a few steps in hopes to retreat back towards the group. "Bye, J.K." He managed one last grin, then fully turned around.

In all of the time I had known Zeke, I had never seen him runaway scared. Until that very moment.

Right when I assumed he crashed and burned, I gazed back at J.K. to see her hold the faintest grin. Was she actually charmed by that mess?

I shook my head, that close to laughing out loud.

"I have to head out too, so I'll catch ya later."

"Okay. C'ya." She waved shortly, then started to head in the opposite direction.

I was about to do the same, but then my curiosity got the better of me.

"Hey, J.K.! Can you give me Lucy's number?"

To Lucy: Hey Lucy, this is Clayton Hugh. J.K. gave me your number.

I reread that simple text over and over. Every syllable I seemed to criticize. That happened every time I texted a new person. Eventually I got over it, and sent the stupidest text messages to friends, but I wasn't at that comfort yet with Lucy. I needed to sound friendly yet not too friendly. I needed to sound funny but not too funny where I seemed stupid. But with the first text, I needed to not sound like a stalker searching for her number.

Once I hit enter, I breathed out, then went back to chopping the potatoes for mor. Her and far have been reminding me constantly of Lucy, her sleepwalking, and if she was single or not. I appreciated their interest in my new friend, but ever since they met the Walkers they became obsessed. Neither of them would have admitted to wanting another couple as friends, but since coming to America their social lives had died down.

Mr. Walker had been over at my house at least twice a day since Sunday, to either help far with some work around the house, or to sample wines with them.

When mor wasn't working she would "call up" Mrs. Walker and they would gossip about too many things. It was as if their blossoming friendship was taking off way before Lucy and I's.

To our credit though, we have been crossing greetings in class and in the halls. That was a step, right?

From Lucy: Hi, Clayton. What's uip?

From Lucy: *ump

From Lucy: *UP. Geez.

I smirked down at my phone, capturing the attention of mor. She peered over and poked my chest. "What's so funny that you're smiling?" She caught the I.D. name even though I moved my phone out of view. "Ah, Lucy." She clicked her tongue. "I like this Lucy. You should go out with her."

"Mor." I scoffed. "I'm not even interested in her like that. Just because you guys had a love-at-first-sight moment with Mr. and Mrs. Walker doesn't mean I did with Lucy." My nose scrunched. "Plus I barely even know her... So, that's why I want to be friends. Quit pressuring me."

Another click of her tongue. "Fine, fine."

To Lucy: Typos are my nemesis too, no worries. Have you started on the chemistry homework yet?

I had finished my homework right after school, and I could care less about the subject of homework, but I needed small talk.

To Lucy: Also I am not asking so I can ask for your answers. Only bicurious.

My heart nearly leaped out of my chest. Why couldn't texting be on my side this once? No, it wasn't the texting part; it was Zeke and Mateo breaking my previous phone which barely caused me that amount of trouble.

My thumbs couldn't keep up.

To Lucy: CURIOUS, I MEANT CURIOUS. I am in fact 100% straight. I am not curious in that area...

Thankfully I had the chance to invest my anxiety after that mess into cooking dinner. The menu was roast beef and oven roasted potatoes, which was a typical meal for the Hugh household. Mor said we had it so much because it was Norwegian native, but I knew she preferred it over other foods since it was simple. Well, simple enough for her.

I had finished setting out the plates and utensils when my phone quacked. Dropping the last fork in it's place I swung my phone out of my pocket, my lip captured between my teeth. I was starting to think she would never reply back.

From Lucy: I guess we have more in common than I first thought. Welcome to the Prone to Typos Club. I'm Lucy, the president.

"She's funny, too. Liking her more by the second." Mor's voice startled me, nearly causing me to lose the grip on my phone. What a little sneak she was. "What?!"

Scratch what I said before. Courtney is far more tolerable than my parents at certain instances. Right now my parents were the insufferable ones.

"Mor, la meg vaere alene (mom, leave me alone)!"

She rambled on in Norwegian about how I could trust her with my true feelings about everything - especially with my love life. Also how she only wanted the best for me.

"Can you not be so sneaky then? That is definitely for my well being." I rolled my eyes, heading into the living room away from my family. I hopped onto the couch, my attention back to my phone.

To Lucy: What does it take to become apart of the council board?

Her reply was immediate. From Lucy: Hm… Not much. Just show up to the first meeting, and you can be the vice president.

I loved how she was going along with the scenario. Neither Mateo or Zeke played along with my texts.

To Lucy: How about the first meeting be tomorrow at Shakers? Around eight?

Lucy took a lot longer to respond that time around. It made me grip my phone tighter. A part of me feared she would turn me down on the friendly get together, but finally she answered.

From Lucy: Sounds good. I've been wanting a cheesecake Oreo shake for so long.

My hand covered my heart. That was my all time favorite shake, and very few people ever enjoyed it.

To Lucy: Lucy Walker, I can tell this is the start of a wonderful friendship.

Chapter 7

LUCY

What was I thinking?

No, that was the very problem - I wasn't thinking when I threw that ball.

"Oh, gosh, Jacob. I'm so sorry." My hand flew over my mouth, masking the pure shame on my face. The baseball was now rolling down the driveway, taunting me every inch it moved.

My brother shook his head, his typical relaxed smile gleaming in the sunlight. For a guy who has been through one hell of a year, he never failed to be in a pitcher mood. If I were in his shoes I probably wouldn't even find the energy to do daily things, yet alone drive back into town and throw around a baseball with my little sister.

"It's okay. I'll get it." Jacob started. I frowned. "Ugh, no, Lucy. You don't have to get it." I ignored him and ran over to get the ball. "I am perfectly capable of getting a ball, you know?"

I held the ball tight on my hand before throwing it back to him. Of course I knew he could get the ball. Jacob Walker was the type of guy who could do anything his heart desired. But that still didn't mask the possibility of him falling down.

"I might be disabled-"

"- but you're not unable." I finished for him, a soft curve glossing my features.

Jacob picked up his right foot, his eyes twinkling. "I can even stand on it without losing my balance. Cool, huh?" We both stared down at his prosthetic leg as he did exactly what he described. He really was getting the hang of things. "Soon I'll put a knife at the end and I'll be some bad ass ninja or something - doing all these kick shots."

Far too excited for his own good, Jacob buckled. My heart skipped one too many beats, even after he settled himself back on two legs.

"But for now," he breathed out, " I think I will stick to getting my degree."

Oh how much I missed him.

I chuckled. "How is school going, by the way?"

Jacob has only been away for college one semester even though he is twenty-one. After he graduated high school he made the impulse decision to join the military, so that took up a good year and a half of his life. He might have even remained in the army longer if it weren't for the accident, but things changed. Jacob hated abrupt change, I knew that, but he never once showed it. Like I said, that lazy grin was stuck like glue.

He brushed the back of his hair down. "It's… going. Forget about school, though. I did not come back home just so you can question how I'm doing in school!" Jacob threw the baseball back towards me, faster than I anticipated. I still caught it, which made me beam a little brighter. "But as your older brother, I have the right to ask you about this Clinton guy mom and dad keep telling me about."

Instinctively I corrected him, "It's Clayton."

"Oh! So there is a guy."

I threw the ball, aiming for his face. Of course he caught it expertly. "No, there isn't! He is just a friend, Jacob." His look of disbelief made be roll my eyes. "Come on, throw the dang ball back."

He smirked. "Since when have you ever liked baseball? Last time I checked you thought the game was boring." I scoffed. "Then again that was three years ago."

"Exactly."

"Or maybe it has to do with the fact Clinton plays baseball for your school?"

"I'm done." It was so hard not smile, but I somehow managed. The last thing I needed was Jacob pressuring me about Clayton. I already had to deal with our parents. "Make dinner for yourself. Better yet, go back to school."

I threw my mitt at him, that time not frightened by him nearly losing his balance. If anyone could handle it, Jacob Walker could.

I, on the other hand, could barely handle talking about Clayton Hugh, yet alone go in battle and lose a limb.

"What are you even talking about? You weren't going to cook dinner to begin with. Dad told me about you going on a date with Clinton tonight or something." He followed behind me, testing my patience. "That's right, brothers knows everything."

"Just like how I know you and Veronica ended over a month ago." I whipped around, the edge in my face faltering due to his silly face. "Even though I clearly heard you tell mom and dad you guys were becoming serious."

He shushed me immediately. "No need to talk about that. It's complicated."

"Then there is no need to talk about Clayton, and the friendly get together we're having tonight." I gave him a pointed look. "Got it?"

The power of social media was a glorious thing. Veronica was Jacob's girlfriend for about four months, and my parents adored her. They really felt she was the rock keeping him together. Turns out he was the rock all along, and when he broke it off with her, she ranted through Twitter and Instagram. She blocked me after I had enough evidence saved onto my phone.

How did I know it would come in handy? Because Jacob was my brother, and I knew him inside and out.

"Deal," he finally grumbled.

To distract myself away from that friendly-get-together-that-meant-nothing with Clayton, I drowned myself in my homework. School has, and always will, overwhelm me in a way no boy can recreate. Though, Jacob does take the second slot by far. Every fifteen minutes he would pop his head through the door, his lips spread ear to ear.

Then when it reached seven and I started getting ready for Shakers, his smile turned into a smirk.

"I see you are straightening your hair." Jacob stated the obvious. I continued humming to the radio. "I bet Clinton will like it a whole bunch."

Before I had a chance to bark at him, the child shut the door and scattered.

Lacing my fingers through the last strand of hair I straightened, I focused my mind on warm sensation tingling my fingers. Was Jacob right? Would Clayton like my hair straightened?

I barely ever brushed my hair, yet alone straightened it. J.K. always gave me flack for not brushing, but my hair never needed it unless I went through a room full of fans or had someone purposely tangle it together. But that felt like a special occasion. Well, as special as a friendly get together can get. So I had to go above and beyond and straighten it.

There was nothing wrong with wanting to impress yourself. It just so happens there might have been a chance of me impressing a guy as well. Purely coincidental.

And so I left the house with the impression that I was flaming-wings-hot. The kind of hot you need ranch for to make it through the meal.

Well, that was what J.K. told me after I texted her a picture, at least. Whether a guy would actually think that - yeah, that was a whole other story.

"Okay you have your phone, right?" My dad asked once he parked in front of Shakers. It was nearly eight so I had no time for his shenanigans, so I nodded quickly. "Your pepper spray?" Dear lord. Another nod. "Let me check your bag and make sure you don't have condoms in them. I know boys are all about that and --"

"Dad!" I gasped. "I am going to hang out with a friend. This is no different than me hanging out with J.K., Abby, or Cara!"

His hands flew up like a white flag. "I was just making sure. Don't let boys take advantage of you."

"Alright, alright. I gotta go now. I'll text you when to come and get me."

Thankfully he didn't ask if I had my rape whistle, because I had left it at home purposely. He gave it to me yesterday once I told them my plans, and while at the time he was laughing as if it were a joke, his eyes radiated seriousness. I had never seen my dad so protective of me. Hell, he used to encourage me to find a boyfriend. Even a girlfriend, as long as she was respectful of me.

"Bye!" I hopped out of the car with what looked to be confidence, but it in reality I was terrified.

Clayton and I have only truly held conversation during the dinner we shared, and while that went pretty smoothly towards the end, our parents were there with us. They were our backbones when things became awkward.

The concrete was still damp from the light showers in the afternoon, so I maneuvered around puddles before reaching the door. Unlike any other store or shop I've seen, Shakers was the only one to have a doorbell. Supposedly if you know the secret rhythm, you get their special edition milkshake. What that milkshake was, I had no idea, but there were rumors for sure. Also depending on where you were standing you could catch the waft of strawberries, chocolate, and vanilla. It was intoxicating.

I pressed my hair behind my ears while skimming around Shakers. There were plenty of people, but no Clayton. I loosened the grip on my skirt, a touch of edge easing off.

I seated myself down at the table in the corner so I could watch the shakers work their magic behind the counter. Sometimes I would bring a notepad and pend and write down what they did in hopes to recreate their delicious shakes.

My phone laid out patiently on the table so if Clayton were to text me I would get it right away.

When I entered Shakers it was exactly eight.

When the first waiter came to my table it was exactly 8:14.

I dismissed him, telling him I was waiting for someone to come.

Then after another fifteen minutes, a second waitress swung around, asking me if I had ordered yet. By then I was frowning, but I tried my best to put up a front.

"No, I am waiting for someone. He should be here any second though." My heart was straining.

Thirty minutes late and no message?

The waitress gave me a sympathetic smile. "Okay, honey. Call me over if you need me."

And so I sat there. Another fifteen minutes rolled by, and soon enough it was nearly nine o'clock.

Maybe Clayton Hugh wasn't as much as a gentleman as I first thought. Maybe he and his friends thought it would be funny to mess with the sleepwalker girl to get a good laugh.

My chest was starting to feel tight.

"Um, miss!"

The waitress from before turned around, her cherry lips wide. "Ready to order?"

At least my good ole' Oreo milkshake would be my company. To be honest that was better than any other guy's company.

"Yes, please. I'd like an Oreo milkshake with no cherry." I handed her the menu I had been clenching on to for so long. Looked like I was back to my skirt. "Thank you."

In record time she returned back with my shake. There were two dollops of whip cream at the top, and by the look on her face I knew it was out of pity.

I didn't deserve pity though. I should have known better than think a guy like Clayton Hugh would ever spend time outside of school with me. I figured he was probably out there partying it up like the big shot he was. Maybe even kissing any girl of his choosing. A girl that was definitely not me.

Right when I though hope was lost, and I was well into Mr. Oreo and his deliciousness, Clayton stormed into Shakers in his practice uniform, his eyes casting over the place briefly before setting on me in the corner.

I was filled with so much relief.

He didn't stand me up.

As he made his way over, I couldn't help but notice his baseball pants were covered in dirt, but as he drew closer his cleats were even dirtier.

"Oh my gosh, Lucy. I'm so sorry. Coach made us stay way longer than planned and I had to fill out paperwork for volunteer work later next week - you know, the mini league baseball tournament being hosted at our school? Of course you don't know that -" He wiped the sweat off his face, in the process making the dirt from his hands leave spots. "Sorry. . . I ramble when I am. . . Frustrated. Overwhelmed. Embarrassed." He scoffed. "So basically I ramble twenty-four-seven."

I placed the straw between my lips. Only Clayton could make sweat and dirt look so attractive. He could ramble on for hours and I would be perfectly content.

He didn't need to know that, though. I was supposed to be agitated. A minute or so ago I definitely was, but the fact he showed up was enough to make me smile again.

"No worries." I shrugged.

Clayton shook his head. "No, this isn't okay. And you already paid? Ugh - I'm failing miserably tonight."

"Really, it is okay," I attempted to squeak out again.

Clayton probably would have told me it wasn't again, but an employee of Shakers stood behind him, grabbing my attention. He turned around, a pea-size Effie Williams appearing even tinier next to him.

"Sorry, Clayton, but you have to leave the shop." Effie spoke softly while referring to the orange dirt path he made from the door.

Clayton let out a long, drawn out breath. He was the combination of exhaustion, frustration, and embarrassment - oh, and dirty. How could I not mention dirty?

"I'm sorry," Effie repeated.

If there was one phrase Effie Williams was known for, it was sorry. Even when something wasn't her fault the word would come tumbling out of her mouth. Especially in math class when Ms. Calvin called on her and she had no clue what to do, even though it wasn't her fault we had a horrible teacher to begin with. Or that one time I literally ran into her, making her books fall to the ground, and she apologized profusely.

"It's - ah - God - okay. It's okay. I'll leave."

Effie did not fail to drop a few more sorry's before drifting back to her spot behind the counter.

Meanwhile I was sitting there, sipping down the last of my Oreo milkshake, bug eyed. When Clayton asked to hang out there, I thought it would have gone way differently. Sure I didn't expect him to walk into the room wearing a tux, fifteen minutes before eight, and a wallet willing to pay for every milkshake on the menu. I wasn't mad, per-say, but I was definitely disappointed.

"I'm so sorry, Lucy." He was starting to sound more like Effie as the seconds past.

There was no time for apologies. I wanted to hang out with Clayton Hugh, so I was going to do just that. Even if it were through a ride back home.

I stood up with a jump, taking him by surprise. "Can you drive me home? On the way we can stop by Sonic and get some shakes."

Past the sweat and dirt, red stained his cheeks. "Uh, yeah. If you want."

Again for the second time that day I found myself questioning my thinking. I shouldn't have asked him to take me home, but instead suggest we could head out to Sonic since we can drink the milkshakes in his car.

The idea of being in Clayton's car though. . . We would be secluded from everything else in the world, just us two, and that made little thrills of excitement and fear bubble in my belly. I had never had a true first date then, but everything I watched from the movies made that night feel a lot like one.

I peered down at my phone to check the time, Clayton and I's text messages from yesterday resurfacing.

From Clayton: Lucy Walker, I can tell this is the start of a wonderful friendship.

I had to keep reminding myself all Clayton wanted from me was a friendship. Nothing more, nothing less. And while that was mildly disappointing, I was okay with it. Clayton was such a great guy, though he hung out with jerks.

"Bye, Effie." I waved towards the girl behind the counter.

The shy blonde set her glasses straight back on her nose. "Bye Lucy, Clayton. Sorry again." It seemed she couldn't help herself.

As we made it outside it was drizzling, so I took that as an opportunity to joke around.

"Maybe you should stay out here longer. Clean yourself up a bit." I laughed, biting my lower lip.

Oh my gosh, was I flirting? Because that sounded like something J.K. would say.

Clayton played it on. "Oh, yeah. Who needs a shower and soap when you have mother nature doing the dirty work for you?"

His accent was so cute. It made his speech slur at times, especially on any words with the letter 's'.

"Poor mother nature then. She has a lot of work to do."

"Hey, hey. Don't knock my hanging out style. I tend to go for the dirty-yet-orange tan look."

I laughed. "Should I try this style then?"

He looked me square in the eyes. "No way. You're perfectly fine the way you are."

"I'm sorry things didn't turn out like they were supposed to." Clayton pulled up in front of my house, putting the car in park.

We had just came from Sonic but sadly their summer shakes were out of season. We still sat in the parking lot and talked though.

I couldn't see his face much in the dark, but I was pretty sure he was looking at me. "Maybe our Prone to Typos club meeting should be this weekend?"

I could tell he was smiling. My heart leaped. "Uh, yeah. Next time don't be late, or I'll have to. . ." My mind was racing. "--give the vice president spot to someone else."

It was exactly what we needed to uplift the tense air. Clayton might not have felt it, but I know I did.

Clayton gasped. "Aldri! No way," he translated for me.

I loved it when he talked in Norwegian. The way his voice formed to the language was indescribable. It was if the language was a keepsake of his true home. He made me want to learn Norwegian so I could talk with him in it.

Once our laughter died down, my eyes wondered to the time. It was five minutes away from being ten, and that was my curfew on school nights.

"Yeah, I have to go now. It's about to be ten." I said against myself.

"Same." He agreed immediately. "My parents say hi, by the way."

His parents were so nice. No wonder Clayton turned out to be such a gentleman.

"Tell them I say the same!" I popped open the passenger door, the sound of crickets louder than before. "Okay, well, I'll see you later, yeah?"

"As long as you don't walk over to my house later like last time, I hope we'll see each other later tomorrow at school." He chuckled at himself. "The big game is Friday, too. I'm so excited you're going."

He was excited? If I were in my room alone right now I would be holding my heart and practicing my breathing because I had forgotten how for a while now.

"Looking forward to it!" I stood up, getting out the car. It was as if a weight had been lifted off my shoulders, but I wasn't sure if that was a good or bad thing. "Bye, Clayton."

He softly said his goodbye as I started towards my front door. I kept casually peeking behind me to see if he was still there or not, and sure enough he was still there.

The click of the lock opening brought me back to reality.

"Wait, Lucy!" He suddenly called out.

I flipped around. Was that the moment where he would run to me and shower his undeniable feelings for me? The fan girl in me wished and prayed, but my brain told me otherwise. We barely even knew each other, after all.

"You can call me Clay." He turned his car lights on, finally giving me a good keepsake of his smile.

It was easy to return it. "Clay? Um, sure." I hesitated. "Have a good night, Clay."

The sounds of the crickets filled the air until, finally, Clayton responded. "Good night to you too, Walker."

Chapter 8

C LAYTON

What was the cherry on top to my stressful school week? Losing the game against George Ranch.

The surprise written on everyone's face was hard to miss - far's more so, though - and I didn't dare to glance over where Lucy was watching me crash and burn. I stopped looking over at her once my pitching went wild in the third inning. There was subtle clapping from the opposing team, but other than that, nothing. Coach had stopped yelling orders at us and let us trail the walk of shame, one I had expected to take a week prior.

I told far I needed to practice harder that week. I told him and he assured me we wouldn't lose to a team as bad as George Ranch. I couldn't even remember the last time their team had beaten someone.

"Thanks a lot, Clayton." Zeke shoved his way passed me into the dug out, throwing his mitt hard at the ground.He was grumbling incoherent words under his breath, no doubt curse words filled with anger. Losing was not a part of his plans. Hell, losing was not a part of anyone's plans that night.

I remained silent with my eyes hung low. There was nothing to say.

Instead I packed my own mitt into my bag, ready to leave before Lucy approached me.

The last time we had lost a game was last year, sophomore year, but it wasn't all on me. Our hitting was off as a team, so there was no one to blame specifically. There was no doubt it my mind though, that then I was the total blame for losing. We were up four to two before Coach put me in to pitch and then it went down hill from there. I walked more batters than they got actual hits. That cost us seven runs. Seven.

I gulped at the severity of the situation.

"Boys, we played hard today. Whether or not that is a good thing, I'm not sure, but we tried. That is all that counts. Next week we play Dolby High, so expect a tough match." Coach droned. "Practice Tuesday. See you boys there."

Zeke didn't even join the team huddle. He was busy packing up his things and preparing to storm out like the tornado of emotion he was. Zeke wasn't the best at baseball, but he did have a talent at leaving in a dramatic fashion.

"One, two, three. Stingers." I mumbled.

We dispersed swiftly. Or more specifically everyone else dispersed from me in a hasty fashion. Coach was the only one to approach me with a get-em-next-time sort of gaze, but other than that, nothing. Not that I had expected anything in the first place.

What I did expect from far was exactly what I got. He made his over to me slowly, each second dragging on and on. He wanted me to dwell on everything I did wrong so I could better myself in the future. So when he asked me what went wrong, I spoke immediately.

"I threw out my arm practicing so much," I admitted through clenched teeth. "Should have stuck to the schedule, like you told me to."

He nodded his head, not necessarily disagreeing, but he did want more. "Okay, what else?"

I rubbed my cheeks, sighing. I knew exactly what he wanted to hear. He wanted me to admit that having Lucy there to watch me play was the unnerving sore that messed with my head.

"My head wasn't exactly in the game," I sugarcoated.

He probably would have pestered me more if it wasn't for Lucy heading in our direction. She made me sigh from the embarrassment I felt about letting her down, but also from how great she looked wearing my team's spirit shirt.

"We'll talk more about this back at the house, Clayton." He gave me a rough pat on the back with a serious expression. Then he turned towards Lucy. "Hello, Miss Lucy. Tell your dad we need to go bowling this weekend, please."

"Yes, sir. I will." She smiled sweetly.

Right then I wanted to tell Lucy Walker how charming she was. She wasn't even trying with her soft smiles and anxious rubbing of her hands, but she was.

Far left with a wink at the two of us, causing me to groan and throw my mitt at him. I expected Lucy to be mortified, but instead she was collected. She either understood far's obscure humor, or she did not see it as anything. Well, that was until I made it into something. The awkward silence following was as much as my fault as the loss was.

"So, uh, the game. Sorry to disappoint." My lips pressed into a thin line.

Her long hair was pulled up in braid of some sorts and she was busy messing with the tip of it. "No, don't apologize. It happens sometimes."

Another silence fell upon us. The crowd was dying down as the seconds passed.

"Could you see okay from your seats?" I asked stupidly. Of course she could. There was a reason why she sat around there every time.

She nodded as her teeth dug into her bottom lip.

Tonight was just a compilation of failures from the one and only Clayton Hugh. Now I suddenly couldn't talk to a pretty girl. What next? I would fail at driving and hit a tree head first?

"Are we allowed to go on the field right now even though it is over?" Lucy suddenly asked.

My brows rose with interest. "Uh, yeah. Why?"

What she did next was more surprising than the Stingers losing to the Bulls. She gestured towards my pitcher mitt sitting in my baseball bag, motioning for me to hand it to her.

Despite my confusion, I shook off the excess dirt it collected while in my bag then handed it off.

"Why don't I show you how to throw a pitch?"

Lucy Walker was a girl full of surprises. Not only was she an avid scrapbooker and writer, she enjoyed baseball nearly as much as I did. Well, that might be stretching it, but she definitely respected the game and enjoyed throwing a ball.

"You throw pretty well," I stated aloud, catching yet another one of her pitch. The throws didn't hold much speed, but they were precise and accurate. The opposite of what I was that night. "Did your dad or brother get you into baseball or something?"

Lucy gleamed a little brighter with my compliment then smiled. "Actually, no. Neither of them are fans."

I threw the ball back to her. "Oh. Then where did you learn all the technique and stuff?"

She stepped off the mound with a sheepish grin peeking out. It was cute. "To be honest?"

"Yeah." I ushered, returning her shy smile.

"I was never a fan of baseball until I came to watch the school's team play freshman year." Lucy sighed in a dreamy sort of way. "You all were so good. Y'all still are." She loaded up to throw. "J.K. only goes to the games for the cute players, but I don't judge her for that. Mateo is a real cutie."

A part of me was flattered Lucy grew to like baseball from watching my baseball games, but the majority of my concentration was set on her thinking Mateo was cute. Real cute.

I squeezed the ball in my mitt tighter. "Mateo?"

The look on my face must have been funny, because Lucy chuckled at my reaction. I knew we were only friends - barely even that yet - but a little love in my direction would have been the boost I needed to uplift my mood entirely. Granted Lucy was already doing a great job at making me feel better.

"You're by far the best player though," she noted eventually.

The best? That was almost laughable now after the disaster of a game.

Which was exactly why I scoffed, disagreeing completely.

"So what you had an off day? You have had, like, over one hundred other games where you were awesome, Clay. Aren't you the same number ten who hit a grand slam last week, or did I mistake you for Mateo?"

"No way, that was me," I corrected her immediately, standing up straight from my crouched position. When even was the last time Mateo hit a home run?

"Has Mateo ever hit a home run on the Stingers?" Lucy asked, her nose wrinkled in a wry way.

"I think the better question is when was the last time he made contact with a ball." We snickered. "I swear that guy has the best of luck. He walks nearly every time up on the plate."

I was only slightly guilty for making fun of Mateo, but that was in no comparison to what those boys are probably saying about me.

"I don't even think I walk that much."

She was poking fun at her sleepwalking, and I loved that.

"So, about your sleepwalking... Have you ever tried to get rid of it - if that even makes sense?" I kicked at the grass, my once clean white socks painted with orange dirt and green stains as we headed towards the parking lot. "Surely there is a way to stop the sleepwalking if you find the source of the problem, right?"

I watched her with caution, hoping she did not take my curiosity the wrong way. That tended to happen a lot. But when she shrugged, I eased up.

"I went to counseling before with this doctor, but we stopped years ago. He said there is a chance I might out grow it eventually, but I don't have high hopes with that happening." I noticed she was mimicking my kicking movements. "I am not a fan of false hope."

I agreed completely. False hope only made failure all the more worse. Exactly why far should not have given me his so called "pep talk". Maybe he was the actual fault to all of this; he jinxed me.

"I totally get what you mean, but --" I stepped in front of her, walking backwards, "-- what do you have to lose?"

She was frazzled by the new formation we were walking in, but not enough to stop her from thinking over my question. I knew Lucy was a busy girl with school, friends, family, and other things, but she wouldn't lose any of that by making her sleepwalking vanish. It might possibly make her feel better about herself, because I could tell she wasn't exactly proud about her walking. On the other hand it interested me to no end.

"Nothing, really," she whispered at first, almost to herself. "Nothing at all."

I turned back around once we got close to the parking lot, my car not too far away. "Then why don't you try something? Anything? I bet there are tons of methods if you look them up."

Lucy appeared much more confident when I glanced back towards her. "I guess I could give some stuff a go." She bobbed her head up and down. "But I won't do anything medical related. I hated the pills Dr. Elver gave me." Her frown was fleeting thankfully.

"Then it's settled." I unlocked my car with a huge grin. "I'll help you out, of course."

Her silence struck me as a bad sign, since she was on the fence about the whole idea, but eventually she got there. I watched her eyes swirl with determination, no doubt the exact image I was mirroring. She was fragile though, so the plan had to start off slow.

"Okay, then, Dr. Hugh. What first?" A ghost of a smile hid well, but not good enough for me to miss it.

I let out a loud, abrupt laugh.

"I'll have to talk to my partner Google first, Miss Walker. Until then, how about we go get some milkshakes at Sonic before I drop you off?"

"Sounds good Dr. Hugh... Sounds good."

Chapter 9

L UCY

The sun was so bright that weekend. Relentless and sweltering, I was close to believing it was summer all over again - which was fine with me and my indoor preference. I was not one of the foolish people in the backyard at the hottest time of the day working to mend the broken fence. Instead I was the person in charge of twisting lemons over a juicer with a cool, calm smile.

My dad was never the handyman and he was fully aware of that; but while his new bromance with Mr. Hugh came with questionable situations, it also had its perks. One of those being Mr. Hugh and him working hard to fix up the mess hurricane Sandy left a couple years back.

"Jacob can you hand me the mint leaves please?" I motioned towards the necessity in clear sight across the kitchen. The boy had the nerve to think it over. Then he shook his head. "Seriously? Are you being for real right now?" Would it be wrong to admit I wanted to watch him tumble to the ground? "You are so annoying --"

To my astonishment Clayton appeared from behind him, the smirk on Jacob not faltering a moment.

No one told me Clayton had arrived. Hell, he did not even tell me he was coming over; and by the look on my brother's face, he knew he was.

My lemon juice covered hands instantly flew to my hair in full regret of lazily throwing it up in a bun. Without a doubt my baby hairs were sticking up in every direction, standing up in a cheery response to Clayton's sudden appearance.

Was that why Jacob wanted to take a breather outside on the patio? He was wanting to catch Clayton before he knocked or rang the doorbell so I could be completely blindsided.

That little…

"Hey, Lucy." Clayton gave me a smile I did not deserve. It was so beautiful. He was beautiful. "I overheard you needed some mint?" He reached out to hand it to me.

I had to gulp down my anger towards Jacob right then and focus on Clayton. He was wearing work out clothes: a muscle tank that showed off everything I needed in life and black basketball shorts. His hair disheveled and messy already, he pressed his fingers through the small blonde curls out of habit.

"Thanks." My heartbeat sounded louder than that, so I had to repeat myself. "Thanks, Clayton. You're helpful unlike that… Eh." It was so hard not staring at the sliver of rib cage I could see from that angle. A few inches to the left and I could practically make out his abs… "Anyways!" I blurted out, taking in a quick breath. "What's up? I didn't know you were coming."

"Oh, yeah. Sorry about that. My dad texted me after I was finished working out with the guys that he was here and could need the extra help. Your dad gave me the okay, too, so…" He did jazz hands. "Here I am!"

I chuckled briefly before peering out the window. There was still a lot of work to be done and plenty of lemonade to drink; and if Clayton was going to wear that and work hard out there, then I could make as much lemonade as they wanted. The reward of watching him was enough.

"Well, you made it just in time I guess. I am nearly done with the lemonade." I poured the lemon juice into a small cooler filled with ice. Clayton cheered at that. "If you wanna head out back then you can, I'll bring out some cups once I'm finished."

He put up cheery thumbs up then flipped around, shaking Jacob's hand. "It was nice meeting you, by the way."

"Yes," Jacob bowed his head with a sardonic smile. "It was nice meeting you too, Clinton."

"It's Clayton--"

"It's Clayton--"

We both had corrected him, but mine held a lot more snap.

"Right.." Jacob eyed me knowingly. "Sorry, Clayton."

The second Clayton exited through the back door and was out of hear shot I wasted no time in reprimanding Jacob with a hard smack to the chest.

"What?!" he yelled out, still gripping on to his innocence. "Slip of the tongue, that's all."

He was smart in walking out of the room. If I had to stay one more second with him there, he might have actually been on the floor in a matter of milliseconds. I had virtually forgotten how hard it was living with Jacob, but at the same time I enjoyed his presence. It gave me peace of mind knowing he was right there across the hall; either playing his stupid video games, studying, or maybe plotting his next plan to embarrass me in front of Clayton.

I gave myself a split second to recuperate before diving back into the lemonade. I carefully pulled out the sugar container from the cabinet and then went to town. As Aunt May told me growing up, the more sugar you had in your body, the happier you are.

Maybe I could make Clayton so happy with my sugar high lemonade that he would grab me in one of those spontaneous ecstatic kisses.

The thought made me laugh aloud. I could only wish.

I poured in tons of sugar, no measuring cups needed, until I was satisfied with the taste. After a good amount of stirring I added the finishing touch: my dad's precious mint leaves he grew his garden.

He might have been acting like a big, macho man around Mr. Hugh, but I knew the real Andrew Walker. He was the gardener who loved watching romantic comedies over most action movies. He was quirky; which was a reason my mom fell for him. He was clumsy too, but not near as much as my mom.

I filled up three cups and even dolloped an umbrella on the top. After examining them - more like scrutinizing - I placed them on a platter and then headed outside with a start. I could only imagine the beauty before my eyes. I figured Clayton would be glistening under the sun, defining his lean physique, which made my mouth grow dry. Thank goodness I made plenty of lemonade, because I was thirsty.

"Hey, guys. I finished the lemona--" Okay, I took all of that back. I was not thirsty anymore. In fact, my stomach couldn't handle anything.

There, in the blistering sunlight, was my dad and Mr. Hugh, shirtless. They weren't exactly the fittest apples in the tree, and my dad had the most disgusting body hair. It made me cringe back into the door, the drinks buckling to keep balance. Thankfully they stayed up, but my eyes couldn't do the same. The concrete was a lot more appealing.

"Aw, yes," Clayton's voice shook me, but the drinks remained intact. My eyes flew towards the storage unit and did not hesitate to widen.

Nope, I needed a drink. Did it just grow twenty degrees hotter outside?

There Clayton was, shirtless much like his father, but boy was he a feast to look at. The last time I saw him shirtless I was scared out of my mind, but then was different. Oh so different.

A very big difference was him holding a phone in one hand, and supplies in another. He looked over at me to send me a gracious grin before putting his focus back at the screen.

Was he taking one of those shirtless yard selfies I drooled over every time they appeared on J.K.'s Instagram timeline?

After a few snaps he threw his phone down on the grass. "Sorry about that. I'm not as egotistical as I seemed just then. Promise. It is an inside thing I do with an old friend in Norway." I didn't find myself questioning him. If anything I would have gleefully cheered him on.

"Thanks, Lucy." He threw down the wood in his hand and made his way towards me. "You're a lifesaver," he exasperated.

I managed to squeak out a laugh. "Lifesaver? You have barely been out here for five minutes!" He grabbed a cup and wasted no time in drinking it. "But, yeah, what are friends for?"

Friends, friends, friends.

Friends did not stare at each other like they were a piece of cooked meat, I had to remind myself.

So I settled on a friendly smile to Clayton then handed the cups to my dad and Mr. Hugh.

The idea of not sleepwalking at night was practically taboo to me. I couldn't even remember the nights I slept soundly in my bed, no movement whatsoever. What I do remember were the night terrors I had the first few times. Those lasted weeks - months, actually, which made my parents' "cute little sleepwalker" a lot more serious of a subject.

That was when I was introduced to Dr. Elver. At the beginning he ran lots of tests and even tried to get me on this drug on trial. My parents denied that immediately and it was good they did. The drug had tons of side effects and actually worsened other kids' conditions. I thought my night terrors were bad; theirs were probably worse. It wasn't until a verified drug came along that my parents allowed him to prescribe me them. Soon enough I was normal again.

Well, if normal meant walking around in my sleep.

And years later sleepwalking was normal to me. It became apart of my schedule; which made me bite my nails at the idea of stopping.

I admired Clayton's determination in the situation, but the like-liness of actually getting anywhere was close to zero. What could he do that Dr. Elver did not do already?

By the time the guys had finished the fence my mom had come home from work and offered to cook them dinner. She even invited Mrs. Hugh, but she was busy with her own work at the hospital. She had no idea about Norwegian food, but everyone was over the moon to eat her famous enchiladas.

Which was exactly why Clayton and I were chilling in my room scrolling through my laptop in answers for a "sleepwalking cure". That was what Clayton called it. Of course the door was completely open thanks to my dad, which filled the quiet with laughing and snarky comments towards the T.V..

"This sounds pretty plausible." He pointed at the screen so I stopped scrolling down.

Change the sleeping environment for the individual. Whether it be as small as another bedroom or another house entirely, there have been multiple cases where the sleeping quarters left the individuals stressed.

He was right. It also was something I had never tried before; of course not counting the different areas in the house I slept in.

My parents prefer me not to sleep over at peoples' houses, but not many of my friends ask either. My sleepwalking was not the best kept secret, but it was no where close to being juicy gossip. Most of the people I associate with knew about it, but they never talked about it. Maybe they thought it was a sensitive subject, I had no clue.

"It is worth a try, right?" Clayton added, optimism stressing his features. "Unless you have already done this..."

Then I remembered.

"I've stayed at hotels before, so I guess my environment isn't the problem." I shook my head.

His frown was disheartening, but he did not give up. "Okay, how about this - don't freak out on me now - you eat mostly cherries, passion fruit--" he peeked down at the notes he scribbled down on his hand from the other websites "-- bananas and peanuts for a whole day?"

I wanted to gag. "That seems so... nutritious." The shiver that occurred next made us both laugh.

"Then what do you want to try for the first trial run?" Clayton asked, walking across my room to flop onto the beanbag. He stretched out his limbs, making all of his visible muscles flex.

Dear lord.

"Um!" I yelped. He needed to warn me before doing something like that again. "You know what, I think I can try the food stuff. Cherries are the next chips, right?" My laugh was strained.

Gratefully my mom called out that the food was finished because I expected to be sitting in yet another awkward silence with Clayton. I could not speak for him, but I felt that new blooming friendship was off; whether it be because I have adored him since the first time I saw him or due to our drastically different popularity spectrum, but it was.

I wondered if he felt the same way.

"Enjoy your last real meal for the next twenty-four hours, Lucy." He grinned wickedly. "I'll make sure to stop by your lunch table and see if you're abiding by the doctor's rules."

He left me smiling way too hard for my liking.

Why did he have to make this so difficult?

Chapter 10

C LAYTON

"Dude, you're so effin' distracted right now. Who're you texting?"

Zeke's voice was becoming easier and easier to block out nowadays.

His popcorn, on the other hand, was hard to miss.

I swatted the popcorn he threw towards me off, then gave him a snappy gaze. We were watching his favorite movie White House Down for the hundredth time and eating his favorite flavored popcorn. I wasn't asked once if I wanted anything else, so becoming attached to my phone was a given; even if Channing Tatum was a great man to look at.

"No one," I defensively put my phone against my chest.

Kai Burns, a fellow teammate and White House Down lover, chuckled. "Strange how your no one I.D. had Lucy Walker written all over it."

On a normal basis I loved hanging out with Kai. He moved here from Australia two years previous and we really connected from the similarities of our situations; other than the girls loving his accent a lot more.

Another ding from my phone made Zeke's lips curve upward. His blue eyes danced with amusement.

"She is no one, guys." I attempted to set the situation straight. The shine glossing over Zeke's eyes was still there. "Dude, what are you doing? Seriously - no, leave me alone. Come on! Ugh." The two were busy trying to take my phone out of my grasp, but I would not relent. It was no business to them and if I said it was nothing they should have respected that. "You fucking assholes!"

I was never keen on using bad words, but that seemed like a useful time to have a dirty mouth.

"I am a sexy asshole, so I don't get your insult." Kai joked, reaching over after I shoved him hard in the chest. It was strange how some guys thought horsing around equaled friendship. I hated being manhandled. "Ha!" He cheered while Zeke kept me pinned to the couch.

Oh what a sight that would have been if Zeke's parents came into the room. They already expected a lot from us, but that would have been a new one. Actually no - it was no different than the fight we had a year or so ago in the backyard. The only difference was I was on top of Zeke, ready to punch him for breaking one of my video game councils.

"You can come over to my house tomorrow night since my parents won't be home. That way we can have some privacy." Kai read out Lucy's latest text message in a high-pitched voice; the one I never got a chance to read.

The two baboons guffawed, eating up the message.

Zeke was having a field day. "Well damn, looks like you're going to get lucky tomorrow night, eh?" Then he smirked, shoving me while getting up and releasing me.

I wanted to a do a lot of things in that moment. I really, really wanted to punch Zeke, but that wasn't a new sort of feeling. I also had the idea of hurting Kai, but I had to breathe and refrain. He was a cool guy when Zeke wasn't in the room to be a horrible influence. What I wanted to do the most though was walk out of the house and head over to Lucy's because she was better than both of them combined.

"She didn't mean it like that." My cheeks were red. From anger or embarrassment we would never know. "We are just friends." Zeke snorted. Of course he would, he was the one who lived by the whole girls and boys could not remain just friends. "I am helping her with a project, that is all."

"Mhmm," Zeke murmured. "Like how you were doing a project with Adrienne Roxwell freshman year. I distinctly remember walking in on you guys making out."

I went to speak, but I stopped myself. What was there to say? That was true one-hundred percent. The Clayton Hugh then was a lot more reckless and did not consider the consequences. Thinking back on it made my stomach churn with regret. I remember Adrienne being so upset the next day after I said we were better off as friends.

She really liked me, and I - no, the mold Zeke created out of a foreign new kid - used that to my advantage to have an hour long make out session.

"This is different," I finally said, ripping my phone out of Kai's hand. "Lucy is different, okay?"

I was different.

"Okay but when you do screw her, let me know if she sleepwalks afterwards. I wonder if she'd be too tired after being banged to move even a little bit." The smile on Zeke's face was sickening. Who even wonders about that?

My body went rigid; my thin lips opening to spew out a nasty comment towards his nasty self, but I was interrupted by my phone. It was beeping the same noise phones do when someone hangs up on you.

"Fucking hell," I cursed. Mt stomach nearly did a three-sixty when I realized in the madness Lucy's number was called. "Shit, shit, shit."

Instantly I redialed, wanting nothing more than to explain myself. I then grabbed my sweatshirt lying lazily on the couch and flicked the two laughing guys off before heading out. One day they will feel the wrath of Clayton Hugh and it won't be a laughing matter.

"Hello, Lucy?" I swung my car door open and threw the sweatshirt in it hard.

There was a long pause. Too long of a pause. Then, finally, there was a reply. "Hello, Clinton."

I had to take the phone off my ear and cover it up, cursing more under my breath. And there I was thinking Lucy hearing that conversation would have been the end of the world. No, her older brother Jacob hearing it was far, far worse.

Eventually I had to place it back to my ear, a nervous chuckle filling the air. "Jacob…Hi…This is Clayton." Yet another long pause. At that rate he was going to make me sweat under the pressure. Finally I spoke again, "Look, I am not sure what you heard, but I promise you Lucy and I aren't--"

"Hold it right there, Clinton." He spoke so calm, it was unnerving.

I was already holding my breath, so I was not sure what he was referring to.

"If you are at all planning to stick your car into my sister's--" The disgust in his voice was finally displaying emotion "--garage, I will personally take your car and take it to the car lot to get smashed into thousands and thousands of different pieces. You understand, Clinton?"

Cars and garages? What did he mean by tha--

Oh.

"No, n-no! I'm not, I swear." I choked on my spit.

Why was it so hard for people to believe I only wanted to be friends with Lucy Walker? Was it truly that hard to believe I could not have a platonic relationship with her? Sure she was pretty and her doe-eyes were enough to sucker me into anything, but I had some self control. Or I liked to think that.

"Okay, then. We are done here, Clinton. I suggest not coming over anytime soon until after I leave, because I kind of have the urge to beat you and your douche friends with my leg." He was quick to add, "Nothing personal, of course. That's just my role."

He was pretty good at his role then, because I was scared. That smiley, go lucky guy I met previously was scaring me.

"Watch out for your car. Until next time, Clinton."

There was something oddly addictive with the way a painter worked their magic to me. Every meaningful stroke; the calculated swoops and dives; the vivid use of the imagination; and all to make one master piece.

When times got rough or stressful I would always pour my feeling out onto a canvas, whether it be as random as a panda or as meaningful like the portrait of mor's favorite flowers, it never mattered. All that did was the relaxation painting gave me.

I definitely was not the best painter out there, but that was fine with me. I was perfectly content with a eighty-five in my AP Art Painting class.

"Try to add more texture to the socks. These are supposed to be wool, right?" My art teacher Mrs. Stevens asked, peering down between me and my art piece.

I nodded. The idea I had was a girl wearing grey wool socks while standing on her tiptoes. The scale only would show mid calve then down.

I was not sure where the inspiration came from, but once the idea hit me I went with it.

"Also, I see you have some empty space right here. Why not try to add another addition to the painting?" She suggested more. Any other student saw her constant critiques and suggestions as a pestering annoyance, but I loved it. She made me a lot better at painting than when I started in Art 1 freshman year.

Mrs. Steven wondered off to her next victim, leaving me stumped.

She was completely right. The balance of the picture would mostly follow the white canvas in the background rather than the girl.

Okay, what if she had someone else in the painting with her? Someone not on their toes to infer she is too short to reach their height. That would be cute.

Before I had a chance to sketch out the idea in my head, the bell rung.

Sighing, I gave one last look to my piece, then placed it on a rack alongside everyone else. Two class periods down, five more to go.

"Have a nice day, Mrs. Stevens," I gave her a kind farewell then went on my way. She once again forgot to tell us five minutes before the bell rang that we needed to clean up, so it took a good portion of my passing period to make everything meet her standards.

I normally walked in a calmly matter, but the time was ticking. My feet were maneuvering around slow people, but not fast enough to dodge another quick paced person.

"Lucy?"

If I hadn't of said anything I bet she would have continued walking without giving me a glance. That was how brutal the journey through a cramped hallway was.

"Clayton!" she blurted out, surprised to see me so soon. We had chemistry later in the day and I was expecting to see her by then, too. Typically we never ran into each other in the halls, yet alone actually run into each other. "Where are you off too?" Lucy asked, her breathing jagged. She must have come down from the third floor.

I peeked at the clock, cursing the limited amount of time we had together. "Um, history. You're going to English, right?"

Her smile faltered at my knowledge, but she did not harp on it. J.K. gave me a lot more than Lucy's number last Friday even though I only asked for her number. I knew her full schedule and I hoped Lucy didn't think I was sketchy because of that.

"Yeah, so, I gotta go. See you later." She began to walk backwards, in the process shouldering a girl. After a soft apology towards her, Lucy sent me a wave then twirled around not so gracefully, nearly running across the hall to Ms. Baker's room.

She would have made it in the room sooner if a certain guy had not gotten in her way. It was Zeke and his sly expression and all. He gave Lucy a flirtatious smile, then moved over to let her enter. I should have been moving to class, I knew that, but I couldn't move. Zeke was crossing the line, but I was not even sure what that line was anymore.

Chapter 11

There was something completely striking about the way Clayton put his all into everything he did. Even in the little things like sharpening his pencil to its finest point or making sure he kept his glasses neatly tucked on the bridge of his nose when he wore them. Sitting in the back of class had its downfalls, sure, but the occasional allowance of drifting my eyes over to see Clayton cleaning his lenses and listening intently to another boring chemistry lecture was enough for me to forget about Zeke Sams' snoring beside me.

"What did I miss?"

Speaking of the devil...

It took a lot to move my focus from Clayton running his hand through his hair. So much I did not bother to cover up the agitated furrow in my brows. Why did Willis have to be absent and why, oh why, did Zeke feel it was necessary to sit by me?

"The powerpoint is on her website." I whispered back hastily.

His eyes lacked the vibrancy Clayton's had when he met my gaze. They were stormy; exactly how the night before was. There was no doubt in my mind that was the reason for his tired state.

"Uh, okay. Thanks."

I expected more. Maybe it was the bad image I formulated in my head after Clayton texted me the whole night about his on and off again best friends, but I anticipated at least a smirk somewhere along the way. With the way Clayton described him, Zeke was a rich boy coasting through school with the help of his status. I never had classes with him previous to chemistry, but I heard things about him - some good, some bad. Mostly the bad though.

"So, can I ask you something?" He was tapping his pen repeatedly against the lab table.

My nose wrinkled, but I nodded. "You're friends with Jacklyn Kate Jensen, right?" That time it took me a lot longer to bob my head. What did he want with J.K.? "Is she... like -- is she seeing anyone?"

He struck me by surprise. So much I could not express any words. All I could manage was a reluctant shaking of my head. That made his eyes brighten up before they were consumed in the haze of sleep once-more.

We did not talk to each other for the rest of the period after that. He eventually fell back into a deep slumber while I gawked over Clayton and wondered why Zeke had an interest in J.K.'s relationship status.

The last time Jacklyn Kate dated was freshman year with a boy named Finn. He was a sweetheart with a heart of gold; most of their dates were to charity events and sponsor parties. His dad was big in that line of work so it was only natural for him to want to become a humanitarian. However, with that job, comes a lot of moving around. After seven months of dating J.K. had to say good-bye to Finn because he was moving to the Philippines.

So if Zeke was interested in J.K. romantically, I wasn't so sure she would be interested in him. He might have been aesthetically pleasing to the eyes, but I heard he was a player when it came to the girls. J.K. needed to know she was the only person in a boy's eyes and not Girlfriend Four when the other three are busy.

"Don't forget you have a lab write up due this Friday! Have a good day everyone."

I was so overjoyed that class was over, I nearly ran into people on my way out. In my defense they were in the way of me catching up to Clayton before he went into the cafeteria. He sat on the opposite side of the lunch room with his knit of not-so-friends while I sat with my close friends on the other.

To my dismay though I watched as his tuff of blonde hair strode further and further away, soon enough grouping with other guys. A simple hi and good-bye would have been worthwhile to my time, but food does mend all disappointment.

However when I sat down at my table, my Flash lunch kit open wide, I realized how much disappointment I felt from food. What a first that was for me.

It was official: I hated the healthy diet Clayton suggested I tried as the first experiment. Since I cheated the first day Dr. Hugh assured me Tuesday would be the big day. So there I was, sitting at the lunch table surrounded by my friends, eating nothing but greens and fruits.

Abby was not helping at all either. She was chowing down on a mouthwatering burger she bought after her orthodontist appointment earlier that morning.

"Mmmmm.." On a normal basis I thought her moaning while eating was somewhat cute, but not then. Knowing Abby she was probably doing it even louder to taunt me. "Want a bite, Lucy?" I knew it. "Oh, yeah. Your boyfriend Clent put you on a diet."

Out of instinct my eyes flicked around, wary that someone could have overheard that. We sat in a corner of the cafeteria since we had easy access to the lunch line, but for the most part nobody was around.

"Clayton isn't my boyfriend." I corrected Abby; which seemed all too familiar. Who else did I constantly have to correct when it came to Clayton? My ever so mature brother, Jacob. Abby and him would hit it off so well, I could feel it. "We're friends."

My use of emphasis did not make her knowing expression waver. A few days back she had already gave me a long phone call about how Clayton Hugh was not worth my time. He was like every other boy; a horny, destined to have a beer gut sort of boy who would turn to making porno's for a quick buck.

And it looked like I was about to get yet another psychic session with Ms. Fitz. "If your bucket list has date a fuck boy with a screwed up haircut, then maybe you are destined to be with Clayton." Even she could not keep a serious face - hiccuping into laughter while the other girls giggled. The only one left out of this laughing fest was me and my frown.

"Shut up--"

"Did I hear my name?"

I had never yelped so loud before. "Clayton! Hi!" The squeak in my voice was unmissable.

His smile was warm and made my insides fuzzy. Why couldn't he be a girl? That would make everything ten times easier.

"Hey, Lucy." That smile broadened as he sat down in the empty seat beside me. He was so close, our proximity was making me delirious. His eyelashes were so long... "I just wanted to stop by and see how the whole green diet was working for you."

Against my best efforts the frown from me was inevitable.

"How can I put this nicely." I pondered for a moment. "It tastes like I am eating leaves. I like the fruits though."

I was surprised when Clayton did not look worried for my well being. Instead that smile remained bright. "Well, that's good to hear, because I bought this for you." He let his backpack drop off to the ground then rummaged through it. Once he brought out a paper bag, Clayton placed it in front of my container of spinach. "I'm not as good as mor, but I figured you wouldn't like the diet."

My lips parted, unaware of what to do. Was that the climax to our relationship, the moment where I felt it was time to plant a kiss on him? Because it sure did feel like it. I was head over heels when I peered inside the sack, the smell of roast beef making my fingers curl around Clayton's forearm. If there was one way to my heart other than being Clayton Hugh, it was giving me food.

"Oh my God," I gushed. When I became aware of the position of my hand, I removed it and began taking out the food Clayton prepared for me. When everything was out of the bag and I let my heart calm down, I flashed Clayton a huge grin. "You saved me from eating a tree and for that I am eternally grateful."

Our moment never even got to play out because Abby had to scoff.

"Alright, then," Clayton eyed Abby as if she was a strange sort of species. I did not blame him either, she was throwing darts at him with only her eyes. "Enjoy you're lunch, Lucy." When he turned to me his hand grazed my shoulder, allowing the softest of pressures to the cotton of my shirt. "I'll text you later today."

When he headed back towards his lunch table, I was not behind in throwing my own darts to Abby. The only difference was that she used her eyes while I used my ammo of plums.

Jacob was not a fan of Abby. He made that clearly distinctive every time she left the room. He went on about her obnoxious banter and corny jokes, claiming she was too immature for us to be friends.

"She might be hot--" His eyes connected with mine, a sense of alertness to them. "Wait, you did say she is eighteen already, right? So I'm allowed to admit that?"

"How would that make things better?" I asked in disgust. "But... yeah... She is almost nineteen."

Abby Fitz was one of the oldest students at my school, but only because she failed the second grade and had to stay back a year. Although that makes her sound dimwitted, she proved herself worthy of sitting in the top ten ranking of the senior class that year. Abby learned how to push through her dyslexia and become exemplary, making her incredibly mature in my eyes.

"That's so weird, but okay." Jacob continued, the same wrinkled expression on his face. "I don't see how you two mesh. J.K.? Yeah, I totally get why you two are friends. Freaking weirdos."

"Thanks, Jacob. Thanks." I rolled my eyes. "I don't see what the problem is though. Abby is funny and nice. Sure, she can be imma-ture, but that doesn't make her a bad friend. If anything she is an exact copy of you just in girl form, to be honest."

He scoffed long and hard. "Pfft. We are nothing alike. Barely an hour of getting to know her and I can tell that."

I wanted to fight for her case more, but Abby returned back in the room smelling of peppermint hand soap. Jacob gave her a curt smile - if it even was one to begin with - then hopped his way to the hallway to find where I hid his leg at.

I was glad he took the time out to come back home. Before I was scared for him, thinking he was a fragile piece of glass. It turns out he is stronger physically and mentally than ever before. So much I did not feel guilty for messing with him anymore.

Something Abby agreed with, strangely. "Yeah, he looks pretty well off in the physical department." She was quick to add, "He is kinda annoying though."

Thankfully once Jacob stopped bothering Abby and I we had the chance to finish our English project together. It did not take very long, no more than an hour and a half. We were about to wrap up the whole thing when an unexpected visitor barged through the door, the spare key from under a flower pot dangling from her hand.

"Jacklyn Kate, what the hell?"

She was breathing rapidly as if she had ran to my house.

What was so important that she had to run from across the neighborhood and not call me?

Her phone flew up to my face, her screen showing a recent Instagram post from Clayton. She could have texted me to look at the photo on my timeline since Clayton and I added each other, but of course not. That was not J.K.'s style of work. She liked the hands on approach to everything.

"A teddy bear?" I observed, taking in the cute bear's appearance. It was a dark, dark brown with a cute orange button nose. There were whites spots covering certain areas and had a matching orange bow tied decoratively around the neck.

Jacklyn Kate looked annoyed that I did not get what she ran all the way over for. "Now read the caption!"

My eyes narrowed in on the text.

To help someone special sleep at night. Hopefully she will say yes to the note on the inside.. #FallFormal2k15

"Wait…" I kept rereading the same simple caption over and over, each time my smile tweaking higher up my cheeks. "Fall formal?"

"Do you know what this means?!" She asked, shaking me a bit.

I was left in a daze.

"Clayton is going to freaking ask you to the fall formal, Lucy!"

Chapter 12

C LAYTON

As time passed in the U.S., I found myself forgetting about my old friends in Norway. It wasn't purposeful; I still cared for each one of them deeply. The only person I've stayed in contact with is Grete Aalstad, but even then it wasn't very often. She was off finishing her studies while I was there still trying to start over.

"I can't believe it has been two years since you've left..." Grete sighed lightly. "I still remember you being only a few houses away."

It was always bittersweet when we had the chance to talk through Skype. At some point, typically the end, one of us would reminisce of the past; where we were little kids and attached to the hip. When all we had to do was run over to the other's house to have a good laugh or cry, depending on what Grete, the great actress to be, decided to act out for me.

I repressed the urge to frown. "Yeah," my eyes laid low, "--those were the times, weren't they?" I sniffled; not because I was getting emotional, but because the autumn weather was starting to take its toll on me. Grete understood that too. "Well, I gotta go. You're English sounds better and better the more we talk, by the way."

Quickly she threw her long blonde hair into a knot on her head, then gave me a sad smile. "Thanks... Until next time!" Her hand went to salute me, but she stopped midway. "Oh, wait - I nearly forgot. Who is this special lady you're going to ask to this fall formal thing?"

The fall formal? In my years previous I had not attended such an event and I definitely did not plan on starting to.

"What?"

"Your Instagram post from a few hours ago; you hinted at asking a girl to it," she spoke slowly as if I were a child. "Right?"

My hand roamed to my back pockets, patting for where I was sure my phone was hiding, but nothing was there.

Okay, Clayton. There is nothing to worry about. Well, other than the fact your parents will kill you for already losing your new phone.

"I never posted something like that before. I'm not even going to it." I spoke calmly, trying my best to remain relaxed.

Grete scrunched her face. "Then what is this?" She lifted her phone's screen over her webcam, sure enough revealing a post from my account.

A post I was one-hundred percent positive I never uploaded.

"Ugh, I gotta go." My eyes narrowed in on the image of a Halloween bear - the same bear mor purchased from her hospital's souvenir shop. She told me she had gotten it for decoration, but I should have known better since she was never a fan of the holiday. "I'll keep you updated."

Grete only laughed before signing off and making my screen go blank.

Her parents were like second ones to me. They wouldn't have pressured me into a relationship I wasn't interested it, yet alone go as far as taking matters in their own hands. Maybe my parents were getting a message from Lucy I wasn't getting.

Ha! Yeah, right. She is totally interested in me and I'm blind. Definitely.

If I wasn't about to reprimand my parents I might have chuckled because of how laughable that sounded. I was pretty good at reading when girls were interested in me and Lucy Walker seemed the least bit. And so I am completely, completely, completely contempt with being friends.

"Sjekk ut at jeg er i ferd med å drepe (watch out I am about to kill)!" I yelled out into the empty hallway, the quiet response broken by my feet padding along. I peered inside far's office space, then the kitchen, and finally found the two conniving villains sitting around the TV in the living room, the corners of their lips curved softly.

I stood there at first; arms firmly crossed, feet set in place while my eyes shot icy stares.

"Well?"

"We just thought--"

"Yeah, that's where you went wrong." I didn't even sound angry; it came out in a whine. I couldn't hold my embarrassment back any further, nor the hope that Lucy didn't see the picture to begin with. "Why can't you leave me alone, ugh."

I grabbed a pillow from the couch and shot it at them both from their cuddling state. Then another. Another. One more. When I ran out of ammo and felt my point was put across, I stormed out the opposite direction.

Way to handle things maturely, Clayton. You're such a man.

There were times I hated being apart of the Ridgewood baseball team. It didn't matter it was only preseason - more like pre-preseason - to my coach. We had strict rules and tough workouts. Most of which did not pertain to the sport we were playing, either. Last time I checked five miles did not build anything in the game of baseball. We should have done sprints since we ran the bases or something painfully productive; definitely not train as if I were marathon runners.

"Good work out there boys." Coach smacked the backs of those closest to him. Lucky for me I was the closest. "I know we did not get a lot of field work done today, but you'll thank me later for pushing yourselves like you just did."

Yep, there went Zeke off to the side getting sick for the third time. At least I could proudly say I held it together.

Heavy breathing over shadowed our chant to officially end practice, but once we all hit the showers the red in our faces disappeared instantly. My teammates went from dead weight to immature boys in the matter of fifteen minutes while I changed into fresh clothes. My legs felt like jello (along with my arms, weirdly enough) so I figured it would be smarter to wait out the after effects of running before driving home. It wasn't as if I was in a rush anyways.

"Clayton, hey."

My eyes popped open from their momentary rest, meeting an extremely confident Wesley Howell's nude body. It was a typical thing seen in the locker rooms, but that never meant I became numb to it.

I rubbed my eyes with a tired expression. "What's up?"

There was something off about him. No, it wasn't the fact he was baring everything in from of me - physically he was fine - but the way his eyes did not hold my eye contact long caught me off guard. Wesley was all about confidence. "So, I heard from a couple people you were going to ask Lucy Walker to the fall formal." He finally reached over to his locker and pulled on some underwear.

I tried to make my breath of relief discreet. Then I concentrated on what he brought up. "Oh, no. I don't go to those things." I began scrambling. "Just another rumor; surprisingly not started by Zeke." I slowly got up and reached for my baseball bag, ready to leave before the awkward conversation of Lucy went any further.

In fact I was avoiding Lucy all together that day. Even if she might have missed the picture or not have understood it was directed towards her (thank the lord my parents didn't know tagging existed), knowing she could have made me incredibly uncomfortable.

"So, like - you aren't interested in her?" He shuffled his brown hair a bit in attempt to dry it out.

"Uh, I--" Of course not. Just spit it out already damn it. "No. Not like that. We're friends." I swore I said that more on a daily basis than anything else. "Yeah, no."

Wesley eyed me skeptically at first, but once I gave him a reas-suring bob of my head, he grinned. It was stretched with relief. "Alright, cool. That's good to know." The way he said that made me suck in a breath. I knew that look in his eyes. He was interested in Lucy like that. "I've known her since junior high," he added once my confusion became too obvious. "She's cute, y'know. Figured we could have a good time if I asked her."

I found my lips pursing at this; then a slow, rigid smile attempted to delight my features. Despite his over confidence at times, Wesley was a good guy. We never made it past the teammate label, but that wasn't because I didn't like him, per say. He was more into hanging around different people. We did have our occasional talks though.

Like right then for example.

"You like her?" I asked stupidly with my arms crossed over my chest.

Wesley was not shy in nodding with a toothy grin.

My mind attempted to wrap the idea of Wesley and Lucy in my head, and as much as it made sense, I couldn't picture it; even if he was such a nice guy.

"Oh…" I stumbled to find the words. Then, finally, "--well then, go ahead and ask her out. No complaints from me." I even managed to give his back a heavy pat before heading out of the locker room.

It was funny, really. I entered the locker room completely nauseous because of running so much, yet a little thought of Wesley being interested in Lucy made me feel even sicker. I didn't want to be that possessive friend who didn't support Lucy's relationship with guys, but I felt something off. I truly did.

So, as a friend, I popped my phone out of my pocket as I made it into the parking lot. I quickly typed something together and sent it to Lucy, but that sick feeling was still sitting in my gut.

To Lucy: Guess what I just heard from the source: Wesley Howell is going to ask you to fall formal.

Chapter 13

That day sucked. Hard, too.

It started off with my brand new school spirit shirt getting makeup stains on the front (and of course I did not notice until I left the house); then I left my English vocabulary conveniently by my printer, resulting in a zero I definitely did not need; plus the yogurt I found in the fridge and packed into my lunch was anything but edible. I nearly skipped the rest of the school day because of how sick I felt.

The worst had yet to happen shockingly enough. That blessing was waiting for me when I got home and popped my phone out to text Abby about homework due tomorrow.

By the comfortable silence I had assumed my parents went out with Jacob somewhere since that was his last week home before heading back to school for a while. So I snuggled onto the couch, wrapped myself in a blanket, and flicked on a recording of The Flash. I had already seen every episode more than once, but I couldn't help it. The show was addicting and worth losing brain stems on as I watched it like a mindless drone.

I placed my phone beside me on the coffee table, but did not think much of it. Barry Allen was much better to stare at after all.

My mind was so set on how adorable The Flash was in his costume that I didn't notice the shadow casting over me. I continued popping candy in my mouth, too infatuated to care.

I did, however, see an arm literally hovering over me, it's path towards my phone. I instantly flew into Momma Bear mode and swatted the hand away, groaning.

"Jacob leave me alone." One interaction and he was testing my patience already.

His hand didn't budge though, so my eyes gradually went from his anchor wrist tattoo to his mischievous face. Ever since he found out about Clinton-- Clayton, he has been trying to get my phone to read through our messages.

"What do you have to hide, huh?" He asked with raised brows.

I smacked him across the face for the fun of it. That was a typical thing between us, especially when we were younger. He always treated me as if I were his pet so he would carry me everywhere like a rag doll. So eventually hitting Jacob became second nature.

He pressed his eyes shut for one second and nodded his head, taking that in. "If you are going to play like that then." When his eyes opened, and a fierce blue twinkled under the bad lighting, I should have handed my phone over without shame.

It wasn't as if I had anything juicy on my phone.

But no, I am my brother's sister after all, so I had to stand my ground.

Before I had a chance to process Jacob hopped over the couch, half of his body landing on mine, and in a blink of an eye my phone was in his grasp. It didn't matter that his prosthetic leg collided hard with the coffee table and probably left scuff marks; he had gotten my phone and because of that he was smiling like true idiot.

In his attempt to run and flee, Jacob jumped up with a start. "You'll never catch me now--" Before he could balance himself steady, his leg must have gave in after colliding with the table. I watched him fall to the ground - but more importantly I watched my phone leap out of hand, smashing into the floor with a loud bang.

Instantly I flew to my phone's side, praying it was in one piece.

And of course it wasn't. A bad day just turned into a horrible one.

I wanted to yell out while watching shards of my screen fall to the ground. I wanted to smack Jacob across the face a few more times.

"Thanks a lot, wow." I huffed, finally looking back to him.

He was in a crouched position, slowly hoisting himself up with the couch.

"You act like I did it on purpose." Jacob gripes back, gesturing towards his prosthetic leg lying helplessly on the ground. He was holding himself up with the help of the table behind him, but if you were to ask him, he would have said he was holding himself steady. "I can take you to get a new one, if you want," he grumbled out while attempting to bend down and grab his leg.

I wanted to stand my ground and be angry - I really, really did - but my heart fell at the sight of Jacob being so powerless. He might not have seen it as a big deal, but I did. I was being so artificial caring only for the well being of my phone. So instantly I tossed my phone out of my mind and bent down, picking up his leg.

Shakily he steadied himself from another close call, then allowed me to attach his leg back under his guidance. I knew his grumbling frustration wasn't directed towards me, even though it should have been, but instead directed to himself. It was the first time I had seen Jacob so upset.

"It's okay," I eventually said, sighing while I stood back and admired my work. "I'm glad you're not hurt…" It was beginning to be a bit more serious that I liked, so I quickly added, "you idiotic dufus."

He laughed, but it never quite reached his eyes. They were stormy with agitation. I wish I could have understood what he was going through, but I couldn't. That was impossible unless I had been through the hell he had endured with such heroic ease.

Abby must have gotten my message to come over before Jacob dropped my phone, because there was a familiar set of knocks echoing. I gave Jacob a sad smile, then headed over and let her in. I heard a loud huff behind me once the red head was revealed, making me smirk.

"Hey, Abby," I moved before she ran me over. Her eyes were set on my brother, but not exactly at his face -- towards his lower regions.

"Whoa, your leg." Abby bent down and placed her hand out to touch it.

Jacob was quick to back up, a sour expression imprinting his face. "Whoa, you're too close." He held his hands out and motioned around him. "I have a bubble for a reason."

She shrugged Jacob off easily. If only I had that ability. Her blue eyes flashed to me. "I finished that paper for Psychology yesterday, so here it is." Abby let her backpack fall to the ground, then rummaged through it before getting out a crumpled sheet.

I grinned. "Thank you. I still don't understand how you want to get into this field though."

At this Jacob spoke up after he settled himself onto the couch, his leg lounging down on the floor next to him. My work; it was gone. "You want to be a psychology major?" He exasperated.

Abby didn't even give him a glance. All she did was hum out a brief yes, then continued to attending to her messy backpack. It was a strange combination, I had always thought. She was a very. . . emotional person, but never sad or depressed. She was angry a lot. Goofy. Dare I say the epitome the attitude of a pubescent teen with a higher range of vocabulary.

"Problem?" I inquired, popping a brow up at him.

It was his turn to shrug in return. I saw his mouth move a little, but whatever he said wasn't audible.

"I want to become a therapist for the mentally ill," Abby gave Jacob a pointed look. She was being way more serious than usual. "It sounds crazy--"

"Literally." Jacob interjected with a smirk.

"-- but they are people too. They need help like anyone else."

I could tell by the way Jacob was messing with his hair that he was taken aback. The subtle curl of his lips suggested he liked this surprise.

"Wow, that's actually a good way to putting it." Jacob finally responded, then gave his hair one final comb through. "Maybe I was wrong about you, Abby. You are cool enough to sit at our lunch table. Or, in this case, enter our house."

I figured Abby would scoff at such a lame joke - since she de-spised Mean Girls and everything about it - but instead I watched her serious face crack into a soft smile, teeth and all.

I, on the other hand, gagged. "The moment stupid jokes come from Jacob, that's our queue to head to my room." I shook my head disapprovingly at Jacob.

"The ladies love my jokes. Right, Abs?" He cheesed and winked towards Abby.

I was surprised she didn't give him a lecture about how her name is Abby, not a set of muscles. Instead she clicked her tongue, actually playing along with this charade. "Yeah. Definitely. Might as well change your name to Casanova while you're at it."

"Jesus." I wrinkled my nose and grabbed Abby and her bag, then pulled her into the hallway and away from Jacob.

I liked it better when they weren't getting along.

"You can't runaway from the truth, Lulu!" Dear lord I hated that nickname. With a passion. He knew that, too.

I shut the door hard behind me, ignoring the amused face of Abby.

"Your brother isn't too bad, I must say," she chuckled, and I fully knew what was coming next, "Lulu."

I gritted my teeth but couldn't holdback the smile teasing my lips.

"You know I hate that nickname," I said smoothly while sitting down at my desk.

She began to snap her fingers and when I turned towards her, she was swaying back and forth. "Lulu and Clint sittin' in a tree. K-I-S-S-I-N-G."

First comes love.

Then comes marriage.

Then comes a baby in a baby carriage.

I smiled wide at this, but hid it behind my hand. Abby was being so. . . Abby. If I didn't know better, I might have assumed she changed her mind about Clinton -- Clayton. Clayton.

Abby laughed a little to herself before settling herself in the bean bag across the room.

"On the topic of Clinton or whatever." She waved her hand at me. "Did he ask you today?"

That was a pretty dumb question to be honest. Even if I didn't particularly enjoy bringing Clayton up with Abby, if something like that happened, she would be hearing an ear full every second after he asked.

I shook my head, frowning a bit. Last night I could barely fall asleep, my stomach sick at the thought of Clayton actually liking me.

J.K. thought I would be overcome with joy and excitement, but I felt more ill than anything. For so long I wanted Clayton to like me, but I guess I pinned it as such an impossible thing to happen. A harmless crush didn't involve embarrassing yourself because you don't know the first thing when it comes to relationships. How were you even supposed to hold a guy's hand, yet alone dance with them without stepping on their toes.

"I think you should go solo, personally," Abby suggested lightly. "Or go with me because I need a date."

I pursed my lips. "Since you're getting along with Jacob so much why not take him?"

She scoffed at this, then tossed the nearest thing by her - thankfully a soft plush toy left by my cousin - and threw it at me. I swatted it away easily.

"He's your brother. That's hella weird." She fell deeper into the bean bag, her pale skin flushing.

"So if he wasn't you would?" I asked with wide eyes. My mouth was agape and slowly morphing into a ecstatic grin.

"Dude," she paused, "--no. He's not my type."

"You hesitated." I pointed out immediately.

Was it wrong for me to take pleasure in her obvious discomfort. She was blushing for God's sake. That was a rare occurrence.

"No, I was stopping myself from saying hell naw. For your information."

Good. The last thing I needed was one of my friends liking my brother. That would be so weird.

"But do you really think that picture was meant for you? He deleted it after a while." Abby cocked her head, analyzing my expression.

As much as I wanted that message to be about me, I didn't count on it. J.K. might have been dead set on it, but I wasn't.

I shook my head while writing down my name on the homework.

Lucy Hugh. That had a nice ring to it, my inner fan girl thought. Really nice.

Chapter 14

C LAYTON

Blue… Red… Yellow…

Yellow… Red… Blue…

My mind spun as my hand glided along the canvas; the abstract image vaguely showing up like I had pictured. It was supposed to be a dramatized face of Grete, since her eighteenth birthday was coming up and I wanted to send her something as a surprise, but that wasn't going to do. It didn't do her justice at all.

I took my paint brush by the handle and bit down on it while I tried to think of a fix.

"Clayton?"

I turned around briefly to see Mateo standing in the doorway. He was dressed in his running clothes and had his headphones lying around his neck. By the sweat beading his forehead and red tint in his face, I knew my house was a temporary stopping point in his five mile run. Unlike me, he found running fun. He said it took off his stress. I was not sure what rich boy Mateo Raeken ever had to worry about; well, that was until then.

"Uh, hey," I greeted him through a paint brush. Quickly spitting it out and placing it back on the paint stand, I stood up and wiped my hands down on the back of my jeans. We exchanged a brief handshake. "What's up dude?"

Mateo's slight smile minimized. He maneuvered around me without a word until he settled himself on my bed. "Look, I know we're not exactly," he moved his hands around as he exasperated for the right words, "--the closest of friends. But well, something happened today and I need to tell someone. I tried calling Zeke but he said he was busy with that J.K. girl, so, um…yeah."

He rubbed his hands together, popping each finger eventually. His eyes casted across my room until they landed on a picture of our baseball team from freshman year.

"I overheard coach talking on the phone this morning. He was talking to Coach Carter about how we look this year." Mateo started off, his lip being taken by his teeth every moment he took a pause. He seemed in no hurry to let whatever he overheard out. Almost as if he were embarrassed to share it with me.

I grabbed the Coke off my desk and took a sip. The fizzing of the suds were a good counter act to silence.

"He said I am the dead weight on the team," Mateo finally got off his chest. "He said I haven't grown since freshman year like he had hoped and thinks if I don't get better real quick, I won't be able to play ball for the team once the real season comes along."

My face scrunched together. "What?"

I had always seen Mateo as the weak link on the team, but I never thought our coaches would act on it. He was apart of the team after all - flaws and all. Before every game we always shared the same handshake since he was a big stickler for superstition.

Mateo ran his hands through his hair, sighing loudly. "I guess he didn't think anyone was in the locker room so early in the morning."

His eyes met mine. "What am I going to do? My dad is going to disown me or something. Ugh."

"No way, that isn't going to happen." I said with the utmost confidence. Mateo might not have been good but he tried really hard. It wasn't as if he was doing a half ass job. That in itself is admirable. "Maybe if I talk to him--"

"That won't change the fact I suck--"

"You just need to be coached, that's all." I placed my Coke down to talk down to him. "It isn't your fault our coaches don't know how."

Our coaches knew how to train players that already had the skill sets, but they never coached someone a day in their life. We never got better because of them. The little progress Mateo and Zeke had had over the years was because of the extra practice they put in alongside me.

Mateo was mumbling incoherent things under his breath.

I understood why he was so shaken up - hell if I overheard my coach saying that about me, I would probably be too embarrassed to ever play again. Mateo didn't need to give up though. He had plenty of time before the season actually started.

"I can coach you," I said before thinking about it. It was an impulsive thing to say, since my schedule was already as full like it was, but I felt like Mateo could get better. Would he be the best baseball player since Babe Ruth? Of course not, but he can at least be considered a baseball player. When I received confused eyes, I nodded more. "Yeah, we'll do sessions and stuff. Mostly for hitting though," I added in a soft voice. He wasn't good at hitting. At all.

Mateo stood there stunned, his eyes scanning my face to see if I was serious or not. I wasn't sure what he had expected. I wasn't like Zeke; I wouldn't have tormented him.

"Seriously." I chuckled, the silence becoming absurd. "It's no big deal." Okay, maybe it was a little.

Before I went and dropped my offer jokingly to make him speak, his frown suddenly lifted, and he laughed. It was traced with relief and so much surprise. It was as if I made his day, which made me smile brighter.

"I can't believe you'd do that, man." He gave me another serious stare before smiling to himself. "Thank you. Seriously."

Surprisingly spending my afternoon with Mateo wasn't that bad. In fact it was great, actually. That was until he became rather persistent with the idea of me taking Lucy to the dance.

"I just got this bad vibe when Wesley told me he was going to ask Lucy to the dance. Nothing personal against him. . . but you definitely know how guys are. How you are."

Mateo pointed an accusing finger. "Don't forget about yourself. You act like a few months ago you weren't going around partying and finding babes left and right." He took a handful of popcorn and dropped it into his mouth. "But I don't get it; why don't you just ask Lucy to the dance if it's bothering you so much?" Mateo asked immediately, as if it were an obvious answer to my problem. "Would you rather her go with a friend or a guy looking to get it on by the end of the night?"

That was such a good way to putting it. "Alright, I'll go and talk to J.K. or someone and get them to take her." I smiled wide only to receive a frown. "Thanks for the advice, I feel a lot better about the dance now."

"Clayton--"

"I know, I know. Dammit." I rubbed my face with my hands. "I just don't want her to get the wrong idea, okay?"

Mateo smirked. I hated it when people smirked at me. "Yeah, because texting her all the time and wanting to hang out isn't giving out the wrong idea." I pushed him, cracking a grin. When he put it that way I sounded like a desperate love struck boy. "She's cute. I don't blame you for liking her."

Lucy Walker wasn't like any other girl I had met before. She enjoyed keeping to herself rather than going out and partying. She actually liked the game of baseball, not only the so called perks that came with the baseball pants. I had barely even gotten to know her that first month, yet I was completely in awe of the way she handled her sleepwalking.

"Yeah..." I breathed out, finally. "She's pretty remarkable."

His brows raised.

"I don't, like, like-like her, though," I suddenly shot out, forgetting about that delicate little detail before Mateo got the wrong idea.

It looked as though that idea was already planted in his mind though, because all I received was a knowing grin.

Finally the autumn weather was rolling in which meant cool breezes when you needed them the most. Mateo ended up staying at my house the rest of the afternoon and for once we talked. We talked about a lot of things, but they each somehow revolved around Lucy and her sleepwalking.

Surprisingly Mateo was curious about her condition. He asked logical questions any sane person would have - not ones that involved whether or not she would sleepwalk after spending the night with someone. I told him everything I knew, minus the description of how she looked on the night she walked to my house. She was barely wearing anything - something meant for only her eyes only, and it didn't feel right to share that with Mateo. I barely even allowed myself to reminisce of Lucy's tiny shorts and top before hitting myself with guilt.

"Hey you should come over to my house sometimes. My mom's been asking about you." Mateo began heading down the driveway when he gave me the invitation. The last time I had been to his house was a little over a year ago for his raunchy Halloween party. "Unless you're too busy trying woo Lucy. You know me, I don't cock block."

Yep, there is the guy I know so well.

Even though it was poor in taste, I found myself laughing. "Sure, I'll keep that in mind. Maybe next week after our hitting sessions I can go over."

He nodded in agreement. "Well, I'll talk to you later. Good luck with Lucy!" I couldn't exactly tell because it was so quick, but Mateo looked to have winked before he waved me off. Then like that he was beginning his run back home.

The cold breeze began to pick up so I rushed to my car and quickly turned it on so it could start heating up. Then I headed back inside and prepped for my dance formal proposal - if that's even what is was called. I knew I was going to use the teddy bear, thanks to the genius idea from mor, but other than that I had no idea what to do.

This would be so much easier over text, I thought.

In efforts to keep the plan going, I figured it would be best to decide on my way over to Lucy's house. That would give me a few minutes to come up with something without the option of backing out.

I could always turn around…

No, no, no. This is happening. It is.

So I hopped into my car without a hitch - even managed to flick the radio on my favorite station without my hands shaking. I was exuding confidence; which consisted of a composed appearance but shit scared mentality.

Those few minutes flew by as I found myself parking in the Walkers' driveway. I didn't see her older brother's car, which was a good start, so I breathed out easier.

I could do this.

I got out of the car.

I could.

Before I reached the porch the front door swung open and out popped Mrs. Walker.

Abort. Abort. Abort mission.

She didn't notice me at first as she locked up the house, but since I didn't exactly have the speed like The Flash, I didn't have anywhere to go. So I awkwardly stood there, awaiting a painful exchange of greetings.

"Hi, Mrs. Walker." Finally she took notice of me and a smile braced her face. She walked down the porch steps. I sucked in a breath. "I was wondering if Lucy was home?" I held on to the Halloween bear tightly, cuddling it against my chest.

Her eyes went from the bear to me then back and forth between the two. When her friendly smile fell a tiny bit, I knew Lucy must not have been home. "You just missed her. She headed to Panera to study for a test with friends."

Great. That's just great.

"What is this about?" Mrs. Walker gestured towards the stuffed animal.

"Oh, um," I shuffled in my spot, "To be honest with you, Mrs. Walker…" It wasn't as if we were going to go as dates, right? I was simply saving Lucy the trouble of having to with Wesley or some other sleaze. "I was going to ask Lucy to the fall formal next month. As friends, of course. But if you don't want me to to ask her then I understand perfectly. I'm sorry. I'll be going no--"

"Why wouldn't I want you to ask her?" Mrs. Walker suddenly interjected on my rambling. Her green eyes locked on me when all I wanted was to run away. "You're a good boy, Clayton. Nothing like that other guy who asked her a few days ago. Thank the lord she turned him down," she breathed out, wiping nonexistent sweat from her forehead.

My brows sparked up at this news. Wesley already asked Lucy. . . and she turned him down. The strange feeling in my gut passed instantly, but another soon replaced it.

If Lucy rejected him then I had no reason to ask her to the dance. She was probably planning on going with her group of friends anyways. Yet there I was standing in front of her mom, saying I was going to ask her. I couldn't go back on my word now - could I?

"Oh," I said, dumbfounded.

Mrs. Walker waved her hands in the air. "You have no reason to worry though. I am one-hundred percent positive she will say yes to you." She winked towards me then laughed lightly.

I attempted to chuckle, but I failed.

"Did you want to come inside? I just finished making a huge thing of soup. I was only heading to the store to get some french bread." She offered kindly.

I smiled graciously then shook my head. My parents were expecting me back home for dinner since mor had today off. Plus I needed to think of a way to get me out of this mess.

"No thank you, Mrs. Walker. I have to go back home." She let out a disappointed awe. "And if you don't mind, could you keep this conversation between us?"

She was quick to nod her head. "Of course!" Her fingers pretended to zip her lips. "My lips are sealed."

I could only hope.

Chapter 15

LUCY'S POV

Clayton was acting... weird, to say the least. I wasn't sure what had happened, but it's like a switch turned on inside him the past week. He's become ten times more invested in figuring out ways to stop my sleepwalking - to the point we barely talk about anything else.

"Alright, I'll talk to you at lunch tomorrow about what I find online tonight. See ya." Clayton stood up abruptly from his seat, shutting his laptop with a far too cheesy smile. "Bye--"

"Wait, Clayton. We just got here - like, ten minutes ago." I noted, as if that would glue him back to his seat. I wanted to talk. Really talk. Not about different methods to fix me. I wanted to talk about his day and how it's going with baseball and his teammates. "You haven't even finished your shake."

I don't know what I expected him to do or say, but I needed something - anything, in return to not make me feel like I've done something wrong. When I texted J.K. about his strange behavior, she told me he might be going through something and was throwing himself into this to get his mind off of it. It sounded plausible, but why couldn't he make actual conversation with me, too?

"Oh," he finally said. His blue-green eyes shifted to his barely drunken shake, to his seat, to me. "Um... Sorry. I just really need to head home. My mom is, er, expecting me."

My shoulders slumped a little at this. The last time I remembered, his mom worked the E.R. and went in around eight to start her shift on Tuesdays. I knew this only because of my mom scheduling to hang out with Mrs. Hugh whenever she was free.

He was lying to me.

"Oh," I repeated him. "Okay then." With a curt smile and peace out sign, I brought my attention to my laptop. My Supernatural background made me feel a touch better.

Clayton was still standing there, but I dug in deep to not give him another glance.

Focus on the beautiful face of Dean Winchester, Lucy. You can do this.

"Actually," he spoke up, the sound of the chair sliding out making me smile slightly, "I'm sure I can stay for a little longer." My gaze flickered up to his and he was holding his own grin. It was moments like then that made my stomach tie in knots. "Jacob left a few days ago, right?"

I gulped down some of my shake and nodded. It was tough seeing him drive off into the sunset, but I knew Jacob would be back.

The damn charmer even managed to head back with Abby's number.

"I almost forgot; he said and I quote 'farewell, Clinton. Remember what we talked about - or something along those lines. He's weird, sorry," I quickly added, chuckling.

For a fleeting moment his face turned pale and fell, but he recovered soon after. No telling what Jacob told the poor boy. God forbid I have an actual guy friend - who might be my mega-crush, sure - and want to hang out with him. Imagine him if Clayton and I were an actual item.

"Lucky me." He rolled his eyes with a soft smile. Then, when he finally took a few sips of his shake, he said, "I heard Wesley asked you to the fall formal."

I somehow managed to gulp down my own shake without choking. He had stated it so casual; it made me stare at him, bug-eyed. How did he know that? Why did he know that? Why was he bringing this up?

"Sorry," he added sheepishly. "Word spreads like wildfire in the... . locker rooms. Yeah, the locker rooms. He was pretty upset about it."

My nose crinkled at this. Wesley was anything but upset when I politely declined his offer. He had come up to me after school on my way to the parking lot with a printer paper scrawled with the words 'WILL YOU GO TO FALL FORMAL WITH ME'? As much as I was charmed by his gesture, Wesley wasn't always a good guy. I knew that only because one of my old friends dated him for two years and he ended up cheating on her. I could never break the girl code going out with an ex, yet alone date a known cheater. That's inexcusable.

He took it with a smile nonetheless. I thought he had understood where I was coming from - minus the whole cheater label.

Before I could question him, Clayton moved the subject along smoothly. "Why did you reject him? He's pretty cool - or maybe that's just the bro code embedded in me making me say that. Ha.. . ha..." he cleared his throat.

Weird. "Weird," I found myself saying aloud. When his brows popped up I was quick to backtrack. "I don't know, he seemed really fine with it. Last time I heard he asked Annie Bridges a couple days ago and she said yes."

Clayton's lips straightened at this, but he didn't frown. "Oh." That was becoming a habit of his. Oh, oh, oh. It was starting to annoy me.

"Have you asked a lucky girl to the dance yet?" I sat back in my seat, the question coming out easier than I had expected. I knew he hadn't - news like that would have spread like wildfire, not mine and Wesley's situation.

He was mid-sip so I had to wait a few painful milliseconds before he shook his head no. "I don't think I'm going to go." He shrugged. "Not my kind of scene."

All I could do was play it cool and nod. Hell, the dance wasn't my kind of scene either considering I hate being around people, but going with Clayton would make it all worth it. I could imagine him standing there at my doorway in a dashing black suit and white dress shirt - too cool for a tie and going with a bow tie - with his hair styled with the right amount of gel. His eyes would look me up and down, but not in that checking out sort of way. More of a taking in moment. Then he would hold out his hand and we would head off to the dance.

I sighed against myself.

"You okay?" He asked with such sincerity in his voice, it made my heart hurt a bit more.

"Yeah. Yeah," I repeated, "I'm just getting tired. That's all."

Tired of pining over a boy who will never feel the same way back.

Right when I thought we had made progress, Clayton fell back into only focusing on my sleepwalking instead of me. Wednesday, Thursday, Friday - we spent so much time together, but it felt as if we were coworkers and strictly working on a project. Every time I tried to change the conversation, he would deflect it back to being a reason for my sleepwalking, or another way to fix it.

This was not the guy who posted that Instagram photo hinting at asking a girl to fall formal; specifically asking me. I was completely convinced the message was not meant towards me anymore. He was probably going to ask Courtney or another one of those girls always trailing behind him or not go at all.

Speaking of which...

"Lucy, hey!" Courtney Fisher and all her glory approached me with a bright smile. She was holding her smoothie close to her, as if I were accustomed to taking things that were hers. "I'm surprised Clayton isn't here with you," her grey eyes scanned my surroundings and when there was no Clayton detected on her radar, she grimly focused back on me. "Do you know where he is by any chance? I really need to talk with him and he still hasn't gotten a new phone."

I wanted to tell her that he did have a new phone, but I hushed. Clayton obviously kept that important detail out of the conversation for a reason.

"No idea," I spoke honestly. Oh, who am I kidding? He was probably back at his house aimlessly scrolling through records of past sleepwalking patients on the internet. Either that or practicing baseball.

Courtney gave me a bleak snapshot of a grin. "Alrighty then. I'll leave you be. If you see Clayton, tell him to come over to my house please."

With a soft toss of her hair over her shoulder, Courtney slowly moved back to her course.

I hated how perfect she was. It wasn't even that kind of mean girl perfect, either. She was completely friendly and approachable but there I was scrutinizing her every move hoping to dislike her. I guess that would make me the mean girl.

I placed my hand in my pockets, continuing my course to a new boutique shop that opened in town. It was called Sew in Love and J.K. couldn't stop talking about it, so I figured I'd check it out before she buys all of their merchandise. It wasn't too far down the strip either and once I approached the shop, I couldn't help but recognize the artist's signature on the display cases.

Norie Bloom.

She went to my school's rival: Arden Dee High. It was an extremely tense situation between the schools when it came to sports, but luckily Norie was known and loved around the whole town for her art pieces.

The display case had intricate paintings of cherry blossom trees, giving the mannequins behind the glass a highlight with their matching pink and blush tones outfits.

I didn't hesitate to walk inside alongside a couple other people, and when One Direction started playing on the inside, I knew I would love this place. Plus the name of the store was puny. How could I not be sew in love with it?

To my surprise I didn't find Norie behind the counter. Instead it was the boy J.K. described to me that and I quote "was a mega-hot teddy bear from down under".

He definitely was cute with his cheery grin and warm brown eyes. When he greeted me and the other customers though, I understood completely why J.K. adored this store.

"Welcome to Sew in Love. How's everyone's night?" His voice sounded Australian but slightly different. I couldn't pin point it but I loved it nonetheless.

I mumbled out a quick good, then turned my focus on the clothes.

Even if I couldn't go to the dance with Clayton, I should go with my girls. I needed to branch out of my comfort zone. I only had one more year of high school, and what have I done remotely high school worthy? Sure, I started talking to Clayton Hugh, but not in the way I dreamed about. I haven't even gone out on a date yet.

My fingers ran along a plum color dress, the mock neck capturing my attention. It was tight at the top and sleeveless, but it fell down in a parachute kind of form. It wasn't too short from what I could tell on the hanger, but shorter than what I was used to.

Try it on, Lucy. You might like it! My inner self attempted to persuade me, but I hesitated to pick it up.

"Finding things okay over here?" A voice asked behind me.

I quickly turned around to find Norie. Her hair was tied up in a ponytail, attempting to keep the hair out of her face, but wisps stuck straight out defiantly.

"Yes, thank you." I kept it short and simple. I never enjoyed small talk with employees anywhere. I was too awkward for that.

I was hoping that Norie would wander off to her next customer, but instead her eyes met where my gaze went back to. "Hmmm," she hummed quietly, "this would look great on you." She took things one step further than I ever could and picked it up off the rack, sizing it up to my body. "You should try this on!"

I shook my head sheepishly, mouth ajar but as silent as can be.

Norie insisted. "If you're looking for a dress for that dance, this is the one for you. It's even forty percent off for twenty-five! That's a steal in my opinion."

I wasn't sure if she was just trying to make a sale or actually help me out, but the more I glanced between the dress and her, the idea of me wearing that in front of Clayton made excited. So I quietly took the dress from her then headed towards the dressing rooms, where Norie gleefully unlocked a door for me.

My image in the mirror made me frown. I looked plain. Too Mary Jane. Don't get me wrong I had confidence in myself- maybe not the most, but it was there - but I wanted to look special. Maybe then Clayton would notice me… in a way as more than just a friend.

And once I slipped the dress on and imagined my hair curled and my makeup done, I could almost picture myself slow dancing with Clayton… Getting lost in his eyes…

"Everything okay in there?"

With one last glimpse at myself, I sighed. Not the sort of hopeless sigh either. The kind that made me feel relaxed and at peace.

Then slowly my voice came back to me. "Yeah. Everything is perfect."

Until everything suddenly wasn't.

Chapter 16

C LAYTON

"Hey, man, are you alright? You've been distracted a lot today."

Mateo had to touch my knee with his baseball bat for me fall out of my trance. It seemed like the longer I went without contacting Lucy, the more I daydreamed. It had only been three days though. I shouldn't have been so affected by her absence. Especially since I was the one causing her absence.

I played it cool with a shrug. "No, I'm fine. But hey, make sure to place more weight on your back foot before swinging on a curveball."

I don't know why I was doing that to myself. Lucy had done nothing wrong for me to ignore her messages and snapchats. In fact, she had done everything right. But maybe that was the problem. The last time I had ever felt so close to a girl was with Grete back when I lived in Norway. She was my best friend and I had to say goodbye to her when I decided to move here. Maybe I was saving myself from the heartbreak waiting to happen with Lucy.

"That's bull shit and you know it, but okay." Mateo simply shook his head towards me.

It had been dark out for hours, but that didn't stop us from training. It was verging on two in the morning but I had immersed myself in coaching in attempt to take my mind off things. However by the speed of Mateo's swing, I could tell he was finished for the evening. I had him finish out the last ten balls with the pitching machine then clean up.

I handed him his water bottle. "Good job tonight. You've made real progress and it's only almost been two weeks. That's awesome."

The smile on Mateo's face was a sleepy one, but still very happy. "Let's just hope after a month I can start to make Coach have that surprised look on his face after I bat."

The vibration of my phone in my pocket made me peer away from him. "We can only hope so." I said quickly before seeing the phone I.D.

It was mor. Why was she calling so late at night? She said I could spend the night at Mateo's and she normally didn't poke around when I was with friends.

"Ja, mamma? (yes, mom?)" I placed the phone to my ear quickly. Mateo and I passed serious glances.

All I could hear was the background conversation of other people with my mom chiming in. Then finally she paid me attention. "Yes, baby, sorry. Your father and I are with the Walkers at Bridgton Hospital." She spoke quickly. Just as quickly was she quiet. "Lucy is okay, so don't worry--"

"What happened?" I placed the phone on speaker so Mateo was not so left out. He was equally as worried as me even though she was more so my friend. I guess he cared because I cared so much about her.

"An hour or so ago she had fallen in her room. She was sleep-walking again. But it's okay, everything is minor. She only has a cut on the side of her forehead from hitting the corner of her desk and a mild concussion." She was attempting to ease my reaction to Lucy being hospitalized, but it definitely wasn't changing anything.

I was completely frantic after that. Mateo understood completely that I had to go and said I could spend the night any other time.

"Lucy needs you," he assured me. So he helped me to put the pitching machine and balls away even faster. What usually took around ten minutes ended up being cut down to two.

Mor made it crystal clear Lucy was fine. I even went as far as calling Mr. Walker to make sure I had nothing to worry about. Yet still there I was, honking my horn like a madman, trying to get around a slow driver on a fifty-mile per-hour side street. It was supposed to be a short cut, not the long way to the hospital.

Eventually I made it there, even though it felt like hours. The E.R. section was a little ways from where I had parked, so I jogged around cars until the stench of chemicals stung my nostrils.

My eyes made eye contact with one of the receptionist nurses and I wondered if she could read my mind about Lucy. If she could feel everything I was suddenly feeling and want to help me change things by allowing me to see her.

Before I had a chance to approach the nurse, a familiar voice called me over to a sitting room.

"Clayton, you really didn't have to come this late." Mr. Walker repeated himself. He had said the same thing when we had spoken on the phone. "Your parents just left, actually."

I was unphased. I just wanted to see her. "Can I talk to Lucy?" I just wanted to apologize for ignoring her. "I'd really appreciate it."

I just wanted to assure her that if that gash were to scar, she'd still be beautiful to me. I just wanted to do so much in so little of time.

Mr. Walker had a look of disapproval, but eventually he nodded his head. I sighed in relief. I don't know what I would have done if he wouldn't let me. "She's been asking about you, actually."

My lips managed to curl up the slightest bit at that. It was rewarding to know I was someone she asked about in a time of need.

"If anyone asks, you're her cousin." Mr. Walker winked towards me as he guided me. I chuckled. "Don't stay too long though, son. You should head home to sleep soon."

"Yes sir." I made sure to shake his hand. "I'll find you whenever we're done talking."

And with that, Mr. Walker left me alone in front of Lucy's room. Well, it wasn't much of a room. It was her own little space divided by curtains. I guessed the actual hospital rooms were for more serious issues.

I wasn't sure if I should just swing the curtain open or knock on the nearby wall like there was a door. Either one could have a painfully awkward scenario happen afterward. So, bracing myself for the worst, I slowly moved one of the curtains open. I hesitated, waiting for a objection, but instead I got a soft whisper of my name.

"Clayton?"

"Is it okay for me to come in?" I asked, smiling softly at how she said my name.

There was a dragged pause, then, finally, I received a quiet, "yes."

I don't know what I was expecting when I imagined Lucy lying in a hospital bed. What I do know is that I never would have guessed she would have been sitting criss-cross-apple-sauce style with a pudding cup in her hand, T.V. remote in the other. Other than the bandage across the side of her face, she looked perfectly normal.

"I'm sorry I couldn't get here sooner," I said. My shoes squeaked as I awkwardly attempted to situate myself. Was I too close to the bed? Should I take a few steps back? "I'm really glad you're okay though."

Lucy shook her head at the first part. "No, it's fine. Really. I didn't even expect you to come actually."

She was speaking slower than usual. I figured that had to do something with the mild concussion.

"Why not?" I wasn't sure why I had asked that. Maybe I had hoped there was a chance it wasn't because I ignored her.

Lucy's face said it all. Her eyes moved away from me, down to her pudding cup. Her lower lip slightly stuck out in a way I adored, yet I never wanted to see it that way again.

"I thought I scared you away or something." She answered me honestly. Her eyes, so doe like, found their way back to mine briefly.

I tried to hold back a grunt, but I failed. "You scaring me away? You have to be kidding me." I chuckled half-heartedly. "You could never scare me away, that's for sure." My voice got quiet at the end. "But let's not talk about me, okay? How are you love?" My feet got ahead of me and before I knew it, I was right by her bed. She had just finished the pudding and thrown it away, and the sudden urge to hold her hand took control of me. So, I grabbed her hand. "Are you okay?"

Her hand was so small in mine. She, too, seemed focus on our hands before sputtering out a reply. "I had a headache an hour ago but they gave me medicine for that. I'm all good now. Just ready to go home and sleep."

I knew she needed her sleep, but it was such a danger to her. I had this sense of protectiveness washing over me at the thought of her having another fall. The next time that happened, it could have been worse than that first time.

"Did you maybe want to have like...a sleepover? At my house." I was getting carried away maybe, but it made me feel better after offering. "The couch in my room pulls out into a second bed, so we wouldn't be sharing my bed."

Lucy looked surprised by my offer. Confused, even. However the red in her face was hard to miss. "I don't know if that's a good idea, Clayton." She was quick to add, "my parents would never let that happen."

I knew she was right. Hell, my parents wouldn't let me have a girl sleepover - yet alone in my room with me. I didn't know what was wrong with me that night. I kept getting ahead of myself and not thinking things through.

It's just every time I had looked or thought about Lucy, I wanted to act. Whether it be by holding her hand or making sure she's safe at night myself, I wanted to do something. I started to bite on my lip, thinking into things deeper.

There was an obvious answer as to why I was feeling like I did. And as much as I tried pushing away the answer, I knew I couldn't anymore. Looking at Lucy stare back at me with such innocence, I was so consumed by an emotion I hadn't felt in a long time.

I definitely liked Lucy Walker - more than I probably should.

Taking in a breath, I allowed myself to accept it.

"Did you maybe want to sit and watch this episode of Criminal Minds with me?" she asked out of the blue, the silence I caused must have had made her uncomfortable.

I nodded immediately. My eyes felt heavy, but it didn't hurt to stay with her until she got released.

Especially if that meant I could continue holding her hand.

Chapter 17

LUCY

One week had went by since I went to the hospital, and Clayton was finally opening back up to me. So much in fact, that brief hand contact from the hospital was becoming more and more of an everyday occurrence. Well, as normal as a stomach churning moment can go, at least.

"Is Clayton coming over today?" My mom asked while washing dishes.

Before I could even give her my cheery response of a yes, the doorbell rung right on queue. I hopped off the couch so fast, nearly sliding and falling on my behind because of the cursed combination of hardwood floors and fuzzy socks. My mom snickered as I tried to regain my composure.

You are cool. Cool as a cucumber. I reminded myself.

Luckily, I managed to make my way to the door without my clumsiness shining through, and I swung the door open to reveal an ever so handsome Clayton. He didn't even have to try that hard to make him admirable. He looked like such a cuddle bear with his comfy joggers and t-shirt.

"Oh my God, wait." My eyes grew big as I realized what t-shirt he had on exactly. "That's a Supernatural t-shirt!" I pointed absentmindedly, nearly poking him in the stomach. "Shit, sorry, come in, come in."

He let out a chuckle, but wore the shirt proudly. The past week we started binge-watching Supernatural and I knew he had enjoyed it, but not enough to go out and buy a shirt.

"Yeah, after practice yesterday, Mateo and I went to the mall." He maneuvered into the living room and greeted my mom briefly. "I would have invited you to come, but it was when you were in the study group session." Clayton made sure to clarify this even though he didn't have to. Nonetheless, it made me smile. "But anyways, this isn't even the best part." Clayton slid his backpack off and took out a bag. "There was this deal if I buy one shirt, I get the second free, so guess who has matching shirts now?"

My mouth flew open, gaping as he held up an identical Supernatural t-shirt. I love receiving t-shirts in general, but getting a Supernatural one? That made me ecstatic. Now having a matching shirt with Clayton? That made me beyond ecstatic.

"Aw, Clayton, you shouldn't have." I held my hand to my heart. Maybe I was being a little melodramatic, but that's alright. After all, every girl is a little melodramatic with their crush. "Thank you, this is awesome."

"It was nothing, really." A flash of a smile daunted me even further. "Consider it another way of me saying sorry for kind of leaving you in the, uh, dust last week."

That was such an understatement. After the first day Clayton didn't text or talk to me, I was worried something had happened to him. But I learned through J.K. he was perfectly fine and chilling with Zeke and Mateo that day. I wasn't too upset then, since we weren't an item and didn't have to contact each other every day.

However, as the days went further, I ended up finding myself laying in bed, thinking for long periods of time on what I could have done wrong. It turned out I was never at fault.

"I told you already, it's okay." I patted his knee before adjusting myself on the couch. I already had Netflix up, ready to continue watching Supernatural. I may have watched each season over five times, but that's alright. It never gets old. Just like how Clayton's hand on mine never got old.

His fingers rubbed against the back of my hand. "It wasn't, but alright. New subject."

I nodded in agreement.

"I was thinking... Since Thanksgiving break is coming up and I'll be off from baseball... That maybe we can, like, go catch a movie at the drive in down town and then get food." The blue in eyes appeared to brighten before me. There was so much going through my head in that moment, but that's all I could seem to focus on. I was trying my best to read if he was asking me as his pal Lucy, or maybe, possibly, on a date.

The more I looked into his eyes, and the creepier that got, I snapped out of my school girl crush fantasy. Clayton had been more than nice to me the past couple months with our friendship, and this is just like every other moment we share. I needed to stop having my head in the clouds and protect myself from getting disappointed.

If only he liked me the way I liked him.

"Yeah, that sounds like fun. Maybe I can see if J.K. and Abby can tag along? Then it would be one awesome friend hang out." I said with a forced smile, trying my best to sound peppy.

The smile I loved faltered. It made my breath hitch. Did I misinterpret the situation? Maybe he was asking me out on a date after all.

Clayton ran a hand through his messy curls, a small smile returning to his face. He squinted his eyes at me, the brightness dimmer than what I just remembered seeing.

"Sure, of course. Can't wait."

I truly did adore spending so much time with Clayton around our school and extracurricular schedules, but I was in desperate need of some girl to girl time. I felt bad telling Clayton I had made plans for the day, but he took it without frustration. He told me to have a fun time and to shoot him a text if I wanted to talk to him. He was so sweet and genuine, it just made me want to hug him and never let go.

And so it was Friday evening and J.K. and I made the trip to the seaside town of Livingston. New Jersey had always been my home, and I knew it always wasn't the most breathtaking of places, but the shore line was absolutely stunning. The Jersey shore just got a bad image from the reality television focusing on the partying side of the beaches. However, Livingston held a classic beach that could truly take one's breath away.

The small town contained quaint shops and diners, all accented with a little charm. My dad had taken me hear when I was toddler, and ever since then I became obsessed with the donuts from a bakery there. It might have been a thirty minute drive, but it was worth it to me. Especially since I got to hang out with my best friend.

"Wait, so he asked you to go see a movie and get dinner after ?"J.K. was reeling after I shared my news. I felt like the best time to share it with her was when we were sitting down, the smell of fresh crescents scenting the air, while snacking on some goodies. "Why on earth would you ask to bring us losers along?"

My brows raised. I didn't know why I was so surprised her reaction was this way. Jacklyn Kate had this way of seeing the romance in everything. So of course when it came to anything Clayton related, she would see it as my fairy tale coming true.

"You know he doesn't like me like that," I started.

She scowled at me. "A guy doesn't put as much effort as he is if he doesn't at least like you the slightest bit. Have you forgotten how bad he was before? He was the party and hook-up-with-multiple-girls type."

That always bothered me in the back of my mind. Clayton Hugh was such a great guy now, be had done some bad things. I knew about some of his drinking tendencies and that he had smoked many things before through talk at school, but I always hoped that wasn't true. Morally, I didn't plan on drinking alcohol or smoking. And to be honest, the idea of ever being with someone who thought smoking anything was acceptable bothered me.

"Yes. . . I know. But --"

"I refuse to go to this night out with y'all. So does Abby!" She bit into her donut dramatically.

I frowned. "You don't even know if Abby would like to or not."

J.K. clicked her tongue. "Nope, nope. You are going to go in this alone, and see how it goes. If he ends up paying for you, it's a date. If he ends up holding your hand or putting his arm around you during the movie, it's a date. If he tries to impress you with a fairly nice restaurant for dinner, it's a date. And lastly, if he gives you a goodnight kiss, it's a date."

Her hazel eyes bored into mine, full of intensity. I admired how passionate she was about my love life, but I didn't need to be let down. I nodded my head in hopes to changing the subject, but didn't plan on believing that any of those things would happen.

Then the perfect subject changer popped into mind. "So have you still be talking to Zeke?"

The mention of Zeke always made me feel uncomfortable. I never knew whether to like him or dislike him, and according to Clayton, that was a regular feeling when it came to the boy. And by the look on J.K.'s face, she knew that feeling as well.

She blew out a breath. "I guess. He is just a little hot and cold sometimes. Like he will try really hard to impress me, then ignore me for a few days." Her frown said it all. "I don't know if it's just his style of landing a lady, but I really don't enjoy it."

I processed this information - trying to without bias - and shook my head. If Zeke wanted to have a good relationship with Jacklyn Kate and not some off and on again type of fling, he needed to get his head out of his ass.

"I don't like him." I stated matter-of-factly.

J.K. shrugged a little, not defending him the slightest bit. "He isn't the best guy..."

"Then why are you still talking to him?" I leaned in, watching as J.K.'s face fell.

I had an idea as to why she was putting herself through all this trouble. After her last relationship with Finn ended with him moving to a different country, she hasn't been the same. She had grown very close to him, and I thought that they would never break up. But life takes its course and they had to part ways. I was thinking that maybe J.K. was holding on to the idea of her and Zeke because she felt like he could turn around. And maybe he could, but he needed to that as soon as possible because there was only so much games a girl can take.

"You don't know him how I do. He can be really sweet when he tries to be. I feel like he could surprise a lot of people one day." She was very serious, but her face was lightened with a tiny smile.

I didn't have anything further to say, so I just bobbed my head.

It looked to be her time to change the subject. "But yeah, back to you and Clayton." Oh, joy. "Have you thought about asking him to go to the dance with you as a friend? You guys are starting to get really close. And whether that be platonically or romantically, I have no clue honestly, I think it would be fun for y'all to go together."

We started to get up and clean our table. She nudged me with her elbow. "It wouldn't hurt to go with him as a friend, right?"

This wasn't the first time that thought crossed through my mind. Originally with the whole dance situation where I thought he was going to ask me, I threw the idea in the trash. Especially since he told me the dances weren't his style. But the more I thought about it, the more the idea seemed okay. It wouldn't harm our friendship at all.

I gave J.K. a sly smile. "That may be a good idea."

Her whole face brightened up with a grin. She even squealed a little too. "You guys would be the cutest couple there, to be honest."

I blushed at the idea.

We really would be cute.

This wasn't a good plan to me anymore. It was a great one.

Chapter 18

C LAYTON

I tried really hard not to overthink what Lucy had told me. Really, really hard. But it still repeated in my head over and over. Maybe I can see if J.K. and Abby can tag along? Then it would be one awesome friend hang out. Friend, friend, friend. Although it sounded arrogant, I had never been friendzoned by a girl I was interested in before. I was typically the one doing the friendzoning, but as polite as I could. I never wanted to hurt girls' feelings after all.

So there I was, tapping a pencil on my chin as my teacher droned about yet another boring lecture, thinking about it again.

In the end Lucy had texted me saying J.K. and Abby couldn't make it, but that only made me so happy. I would have been ecstatic if she hadn't of asked them in the first place to come. Maybe my intentions weren't clear enough with the matching t-shirts or wanting to spend as much time during the day with her, but I thought it was noticeable something had changed with how I felt about her.

What else did I have to do?

Of course there was the obvious option: I could confess my profound liking for her. Normally I wouldn't be so timid with my feelings about a girl. However, Lucy was different than any other girl I had met. She was quite the opposite of all the American girls I either hooked up with or tried to go on a date with. Granted, I never had good taste in seeking out a girl who was actual girlfriend material. But then I thought my luck had changed. Lucy was the type of girl any guy would want to snatch up and call his.

Yet the idea of telling her all of this shook me to no end.

I was too nervous about telling her in the fear of being rejected and harming our still forming friendship.

"Clayton, what do you think about the quote?"

My teacher snapped me out of my head and back to Earth I crashed.

When I couldn't give a response of any kind (not even a simple "uhhhh"), she shook her head and moved on to someone else. Whoops.

Luckily it was my last class of the day, and I only had to sit through another fifteen minutes. Of course that time felt infinitely longer, but somehow I pulled through without losing my head. The bell rang and I instantly flew out of the room just like that. I was supposed to have baseball practice that day since it was a Thursday, but I had told Coach Carter that I had some family matters to attend to.

"Hey, Lucy!"

Okay, maybe I had lied.

I was out of breath from running down the set of stairs to the front entrance. Lucy's last period was as a librarian assistant and she is normally one of the first people to exit the school. But not that day; I had to see her.

A smile graced her face which made me hold my own.

She had such a pretty smile. . .

"Clayton, hey." She sounded surprised, and I didn't blame her. She knew I was supposed to be heading out to the field by then.

I opened the door for her. "So it turns out I'm not practicing today. Did you maybe want to catch that movie tonight?" My face was beginning to get hot. "Just us though."

Lucy's gaze at her phone snapped to me, and for a moment it felt like déjà vu to when we first officially met outside of school at that record store.

"Oh. ." She began, but didn't continue.

My walking slowed down just a tad, the slightest bit of pep I had fading along with my speed.

Why did she look so turned off? Maybe I was over-analyzing her emotionless face, but there was such a drastic expression change after I said that.

"Hey, man, you are Clayton Hugh. Girls like confidence," I could hear Mateo's words of encouragement from a few days ago. When I told him about my feelings for Lucy, all he did was smirk. Apparently he could see that from miles away. "You got this, dude."

With that little bit of encouragement, I managed to pull out a slight grin. "It's okay, you can say no if you don't want to."

Instantly Lucy shook her head. Her eyes widened while her hand grazed my forearm as if she were trying to comfort me. "Why wouldn't I want to?" she asked as if I was dumb for assuming otherwise. "Of course I would. It's just I was supposed to do chores today when I got home. When did you want to go to the movies?"

Shit, I didn't think that far into it yet.

"I was shooting for like a five-ish showing." Hopefully they had a showing around then.

"Yeah, that could work. I'll just race to the house now and get everything I need to get done, done." She began to walk again towards the parking lot. A smile was sent my way along with a wave. "Let me know when you start heading over to my house!"

I was disappointed I didn't get to spend more time with her just then, but it was okay. I was about to have a whole evening with Lucy that could be considered a date. At least I considered it to be a date.

Lucy was already half way down the parking lot when I regained my motion. It was like a switch turned on. I moved as fast I could to my own car, which happened to be on the opposite side of the school.

Before I had a chance to drive off, Zeke popped up behind the car.

I sucked in a breath because that could have turned into a bad situation. Rolling down the window, I had to squint through the glare of the sun to look up at him.

"Hey, man." We did our handshake real quick. "So do you have any plans tonight?"

I wasn't quite sure what to say. One side of me wanted to blurt out I was going on a date with Lucy proudly, but the other side wanted to keep that information to myself. I guessed I could not be so specific.

"I'm gonna hang out with Lucy some." I shrugged nonchalantly. If only I were actually that calm about the whole thing. I was definitely shaking in my boots a bit. "Why?"

Zeke sighed at my plans and I didn't expect anything less of that. "Well, practice actually got cancelled today so I was gonna see if you wanted to join me at a party down in Angleton. The same place we went last year, I don't know if you remember." He chuckled. "You probably don't."

I definitely couldn't remember. I was sure though the night was full of a wondrous amount of drinking and girls and smoking. All stuff I wasn't interested in anymore, that's for sure.

Although I had no interest in attending, I raised my hands in the air with a frown. "Well, sorry man."

"Yeah, yeah. It's alright, I guess I can't blame you for wanting to hang out with your girlfriend." Zeke spoke so casually, I didn't fight his comment. After all that's what I wanted in the end - to be Lucy's boyfriend. "I guess I could do the same with J.K., huh?"

I ended up placing the car back in park. Zeke and I hadn't been talking much the past few weeks like we used to, and I definitely needed to do some catching up. Especially after J.K. was feeling on the fence about Zeke. He might not have been the greatest gentleman out there, but I knew he could turn out better. He just needed someone to whip his ass into shape.

"What's up with you two anyways?"

He began to rub his face, his nose scrunching up a bit. "I'm pretty sure I screwed up any chance of being with her." A laugh came out. "And maybe that's my problem, because the idea of being with any girl sounds exhausting and boring."

He was right in a way. A lot of work went into having a relationship work out. Sometimes it could be exhausting. In my eyes though, I could never be bored with a girl I truly felt over the moon for. We could spend the whole day together just watching T.V. and I'd still be excited and happy. Or maybe that's just the dream world I wished to be in.

"Well, if you don't want to… I think you should just cut if off with Jacklyn then. Quit wasting her time." Sometimes being a friend meant you had to be blunt, especially when it came to someone like Zeke. He needed some tough love. "But yeah, man, anyways. I gotta head home and get ready."

I wasn't sure what he was nodding his head at, but I knew he wasn't done with J.K. just yet. Something about the look in his eyes when I suggested letting her go told me that.

"Yeah, okay."

I felt bad leaving him like that. His shoulders were drooping, face looking as if his thoughts were overwhelming him. I knew how he felt. Feeling new things could have that effect on people. It definitely had it's effects on me until I accepted how much I liked Lucy.

"Can I ask you a question though? To get your opinion and stuff." I started the car back up while nodding. His face remained serious for the most part, but his lips tweaked into a slight, hopeful smile. "Do you think I ruined things between J.K. and I? I've been so on and off with her, and I feel like I've driven her away."

Zeke managed to amuse me sometimes. He might act like he was scared to genuinely like a girl for more than just her looks, but he obviously cared for Jacklyn Kate. "I thought you didn't want to be tied down because it would be exhausting and boring, remember? Was that not what you said just, like, a minute ago?"

He chuckled sarcastically while rolling his eyes. "Yeah, yeah, yeah. But be honest with me bro. You think I still have a chance?"

I began to pull back out of the parking spot, a smirk playing on my face. "Maybe if you take her out for ice cream. I heard from Lucy that's one of her favorite things to eat." I laughed a little. "If there's one way to a woman's heart, it's through food. Or at least that's what my dad says."

All Zeke did was bob his head, processing this new information to him. No, Lucy didn't tell me J.K. loved ice cream, but that was okay. I just needed to give him at least some idea to taking her out on a date and stop inviting her to parties she will never go to and baseball practices and games.

"Alright. Thanks. I'll see you later, Clayton. Good luck with your lady tonight. Don't forget to make your move, hot shot!"

I wasn't sure if he meant that in a more sexual way, but I didn't care. He was encouraging our relationship, and I honestly appreciated that. Approval was a big thing to me and my family and friends all liked Lucy.

The whole ride home I was thinking over how the night could go if I made a move. There were plenty of bad turn outs that could occur, but on the other hand an array of good ones. I would never see if I don't at least try.

I pulled into the driveway and heard my phone go off. It was the sound of Pikachu; which was Lucy's text alert for me. On her phone she used my favorite Pokemon, Squirtle, as my ringtone. We were definitely dorks at heart.

Instantly I took my phone out, and smiled down at the screen. I wasn't feeling too confident about the night before, but her message changed something in me. I felt a lot more at ease.

From Lucy : Just wanted to let you know I'm excited for tonight. I'll see you very soon. :)

Chapter 19

I might have lied to Clayton about having to clean. It was for both of our own good, too, because my hair really needed a nice wash and preparation for the evening. Maybe it was wrong of me for wanting to make sure I looked more presentable that night, but oh well. I was about to glamorize myself.

Well, more like J.K. was going to glamorize me. Let me face it, I wasn't the best at doing my makeup unlike her. She said it was because I wasn't wizardly and that apparently she is.

"I was thinking we'd curl your hair and frame your face with braiding the front pieces back." J.K. touched my blow-dried hair, her fingers slipping through effortlessly. "And then with the makeup keep the eyes soft and then a plum colored lip."

She was thinking big with this transformation, which I appreciated, but we only had an hour and a half before Clayton was scheduled to appear at my doorstep. Jacklyn Kate might have been dreaming too high.

My face must have screamed worry, because she instantly gave me one of those reassuring smiles of hers.

"It won't take that long, so lose the face. You're going to look so beautiful tonight that Clayton would be blind and stupid if he didn't want to snatch you up." She was quick to add, "not that you aren't that ridiculously pretty already, of course."

I flipped my hair, sticking my tongue out. "Well duh."

We chuckled together and then she went straight into her makeover mode. That mode was quite a scary one, in my opinion. Her eyes seemed to bore into every pore imaginable on my face, full of fiery determination. She had that crazy glint behind them, and the fact she had a makeup brush clamped between her teeth didn't help her insane appearance.

It felt like ages passed as I sat in the same position. My butt was starting to hurt, yet when I tried to squirm into a different position, J.K. fixed me right back to where I was.

Was Clayton really worth all of this trouble?

Thankfully the moment I blushed was right after J.K. applied a vibrant pretty shade to my cheeks.

Of course he was worth it. I could imagine the night in my head already. We'd be sitting in the back of the theater, chowing down on popcorn, laughing together at the film. His arm wouldn't slip around my shoulder, but instead his hand would make his way to my knee. His thumb would leave small gestures of comfort and warmth, gliding back and forth across the skin. He didn't have to do a lot to make me happy. Something as small and gentle as that was enough to make my whole week. Then we would go out to eat, and he'd assure me that I could get anything I wanted, no matter the price.

Okay, maybe I was thinking way too much into tonight. I knew I was setting myself up for disappointment. There was still that part of me that clenched onto the idea that all of that could actually happen, though.

"You look so good, damn." J.K. took a few steps back to admire her work. She did one of her own hair flips. "I should get paid to do this, really. I'm a wizard."

I rolled my eyes. "Hey, hey, hey. Quit acting like I was some beastly creature you turned into a princess. I've been a princess my whole life, thank you very much." I pursed my lips into a duck face. I knew J.K. hated those.

She scrunched her nose. Payback was sweet. "Alright. Fair enough."

After ushering me up to avoid looking into the mirror, she did a little curtsy to me. My brows furrowed at this act, but I soon grinned.

"I wouldn't say you're a princess right now though." A sigh fell out of her. "You're a queen.." Then she must have looked at the time, because her eyes bulged a little bit, leaving me little time to relish in her sweet comment. "Okay put your outfit on! Quick, quick. Chop, chop."

Thankfully we already chose my outfit days ago. We actually went shopping for about two hours looking for a good skirt and top combination that wasn't overly expensive. The skirt was pretty and flared out to about my mid-thigh. It was a soft pastel purple, which happened to be my favorite color. The shirt hugged my chest and cropped right below my belly button, exposing a small hint of flesh. It was nothing too much, nor too little. It was perfect and made me feel perfect.

"Now take a look at yourself, girly."

I wasn't expecting too much when I turned around towards the mirror. In fact, I thought I'd look like my ordinary self with a little bit of makeup on. But in a way, I didn't fully appear like myself.

Instead I looked older -- much more mature for my age. Don't get me wrong, I still looked youthful and fun, especially with the berry lip color, but I appeared more like a young woman.

For so long I had feared growing up and becoming an adult, graduating high school, and having to go to college. Yet when I stared back at myself, I felt that fear in side me dwindle the tad bit.

"Wow..." That's all I could muster out.

J.K. held a smirk up. "Damn straight wow. That's my best friend!"

I would have laughed at that, but the doorbell sent a shiver down my spine.

He was here. Clayton was here.

Before I could even press my skirt down and give myself another once over, J.K. began pushing me out of my bedroom towards the front door. My parents were sitting in the livingroom, both sending knowing grins my way.

"Well, don't you look nice." My mom sent me a wink.

My dad just smiled, but his eye looked to have twitched. "This must be a date."

J.K. and I glanced at each other, but I ended up just remaining silent.

"This is definitely a date, Mr. and Mrs. Walker." J.K. blurted out, giggling like crazy.

Rolling my eyes, I headed towards the front door to open it. The butterflies in my belly were especially present during that time. It almost felt like I was suspended in air, falling and falling.

"Hey, Clayt--"

Instead I was met with a stupid smile and boy holding his leg in the air, jokingly reaching out to shake my hand.

"Jacob?" I exasperated.

Jacob crossed his arms the best he could with his prosthetic leg in grasp. "Well, I don't feel very welcomed back."

J.K. thankfully stepped in front of me while peering towards the driveway. "You're so annoying, ugh. You're supposed to be Clayton! They have a very important movie and dinner date tonight."

Before Jacob could even say anything, Clayton's car pulled into the driveway. J.K. squealed, Jacob was wallowing in whatever emotion he was feeling (I didn't really care), while I stood there frozen. It took all of my courage to swing that door open, yet it wasn't even Clayton. Of course I loved having Jacob around, but it felt like he was just there. Sure, it might have been around three weeks ago, but still. I thought a monthly dose of Jacob Walker was enough every now and then.

"Shit, okay. Um, move, you." I swatted past Jacob.

Clayton and I needed to leave as soon as possible before Jacob gets his hands on him.

"I love you too, sis. Great to see you once again." My brother yelled out as I rushed to Clayton's car.

I could hear him rustling with his leg, probably to put it back on so he could come over and have a chat with Clinton -- Clayton. Jacob was known for leaving an effect on people. The whole name nonsense was not one I needed Clayton to know about with me. Whoops.

Clayton opened his door to get out, and I quickly waved my hands in the air for him to stop. If he wanted to not be beaten by a club leg, he needed to stay in the car. His face was full of different emotions, but mostly confusion. Of course the reveal I wanted at the door was ruined. The image of Clayton taking in my appearance head to toe at the door made my cheeks flush. If only things had went as planned...

"Hey, Clayton!" I said a little bit too high-pitched after opening the passenger door. I definitely took notice of how clean his car was. Did he clean it up for me? "Sorry, I just think it's best if we left now. I didn't expect Jacob to be back home today."

I could see Clayton's face fall in a ghastly expression. He dared to flick his gaze over to the front door, where Jacob was defiantly peeking out of a crack in the door.

"Your brother scares me." He finally breathed out. There was a long silence, just with the radio in the background, until our eyes met and we chuckled. "I'm surprised he just hasn't come over here yet--"

"Yeah, he's coming out now. Please, let's go." I couldn't help but laugh. Jacob looked like a crazy person. I knew at this point he was just acting the way he was as a show. Clayton did not know that though.

When he saw Jacob walking down the porch steps, he zoomed out of there so quickly. Clayton wasn't one to drive so recklessly, but I could tell he was a little bit on edge. Okay, maybe a lot on edge. It wasn't until we were halfway to the movie theater that another word was said. It wasn't an awkward silence before then, per say. It was comfortable, especially since one of my favorite songs started to play on the radio.

"Well, that was an experience." Clayton glanced over at me, his smile dazzling as ever. It made me melt in my seat. "I didn't get to say hi to your parents though."

I shrugged even though his eyes were on the road now. "It's alright. I'm sure you've seen enough of my dad for about a year after seeing him shirtless."

He snickered. "Cut the guy some slack. When your mom cooks the way she does, I understand completely."

It was so easy with Clayton to laugh. He didn't even have to say a joke and there I was, chuckling along side him. He made me feel more comfortable than any other guy I talked to. I appreciated that immensely.

The movie started at five-thirty, so we were in a slight rush to make it on time. Thankfully we made it just five minutes before it started, enough time to get some popcorn and drinks. The whole walk in I forgot how I looked and what I was wearing, but when I caught Clayton sneaking a peek at me, you could bet your lucky stars I was as red as I could get.

After he paid for our tickets and goodies, we handed our tickets to the attendant and they directed us in the direction of our theater. On the way there I was hyper aware of how close Clayton was walking next to me.

He smelled so damn good. I nearly let out a sigh.

Before I realized what was happening, Clayton used his free hand to place it on the small of my back, guiding me because I was too lost in my thoughts to realize I nearly passed our theater.

I gave him a sheepish smile.

Before I reached to open the door, he beat me to it like the gentleman he was.

"Why thank you, kind sir." I giggled against my wishes. Darn Clayton and his effect on me.

Ours eyes connected, and I expected him to be smiling or chuckling with me, but instead his expression was soft and serious. His tongue ran along his lips while his eyes danced along my face. I wondered what he was thinking about.

"You're so pretty…" he finally said.

I sucked in a breath. It was a small compliment, but it definitely made me stand up a little bit taller. "Thank you."

There was that smile again. "Anytime, love."

The movie was God awful. Unlike what the trailer portrayed, it turned out the movie was actually a musical as well; one of my least favorite kind of genres. Not that I didn't enjoy people singing, it just became a problem when they sang every single word.

Thankfully, Clayton was there beside me to entertain me. There wasn't anyone else in the theater which had surprised me at first, but eventually became understandable. So we weren't scared to goof off and talk to one another.

Midway into the film, Clayton stood up and sang out, "I'm in a theater and I'm singing!" which cracked me up beyond belief. He was becoming better and better as the days went on in my eyes.

Dinner actually went the same way as the movie. He took me to this overpriced Mexican restaurant, since he knew that was my favorite, despite the fact it was his least. The food was decent, not the worst I ever had, but the main dish was Clayton himself. He was so charismatic and care-free that night. If I didn't know better, I would assume he was putting all of himself out there for me, and I was adoring it all.

"Yeah, this food sucks." Clayton barely even poked at his food before coming to that realization.

I shook my head. "Nah, it's not that bad." I took a spoonful of refried beans into my mouth. Those are typically my favorite, but I made a face. "Well, okay, maybe it is a little bit suck-ish."

He frowned a little bit to my dismay. "I'm sorry tonight hasn't exactly gone well as planned."

Clayton had to have been joking. That night was one I probably wouldn't ever forget. "What do you mean? I've had a bunch of fun."

His head tilts ever so slightly. "Really?"

I nodded immediately. He had no reason to think otherwise.

"Well, that's good then. I'm really glad."

Eventually the time passed as we talked and talked, so the inevitable happened. It was nearing my curfew, and Clayton was determined to take me home earlier than that to please my parents. He wouldn't show me the check for dinner, since I wanted to at least pay the tip, but he would not have it. Jokes on him though, I left two dollars in addition to his tip money.

I don't think one word was said on the ride back to my house. Both of us enjoyed listening to the music, every once in a while humming the words and sending each other subtle smiles. Somewhere along the way Clayton's hand gently reached its way to my thigh. It scared me at first, the nerves I almost forgot about instantly coming back to me. My whole body tingled and it only increased when he gave me a reassuring, soft squeeze.

The moment my home came into sight, I frowned. I didn't want to go back. I wanted to keep spending time with Clayton and didn't want that night to end. I didn't want his hand to move.

"I'm really glad you could come out with me today." Clayton removed his hand from my thigh to turn off the car. We were consumed by darkness.

"Me too, I had a lot of fun."

The crickets sounded through the air as he and I just looked at each other. In the back of my head I was encouraging myself to make a move - any move - but before I could he opened his door. "We should probably get you inside."

I was a bummed, but he was right. I'm sure Jacob would peek out the window whenever my curfew came around, so it was good we got there a little bit earlier.

The stars were extra pretty that night surprisingly. It wasn't too often when you could see so many stars in the sky. I admired them while walking to the front porch, trying to keep my mind off what could happen as we said goodbye. A portion of me hoped it would just be a friendly goodbye hug, while the other yearned for the experience of my first kiss. I always daydreamed about what the kiss would be like, and the thought of it being with Clayton made my heart swell.

Our footsteps along the steps made the boards squeak slightly. When we made it to the front door, I turned to face him. My parents must have forgotten to leave the front porch on, but that was okay. I could still appreciate how handsome Clayton Hugh was in all his glory. At the beginning of the night his matching lavender button down was tucked into his pants, but at some point he untucked it, sort of like himself. He relaxed and let himself go, revealing characteristics I never saw before in him.

"Alright, well." He shuffled back and forth on his feet. "I'll see you tomorrow at school, yeah?"

My heart was racing faster than ever as he took a step towards me. I bit my lip and nodded.

His hands gingerly wrapped around my forearms, pulling me closer to him ever so slightly. I wanted to say something, anything, but I couldn't. All I could do was stare back at his eyes, watching as they bounced between my own and my lips. Before I could realize what was happening, he pressed the softest of kisses to my cheek. I thought that was the end of that moment, but no. Clayton went back and pressed another kiss to my cheek, this time catching a piece of my lips in the process. He lingered there briefly, then released my arms and took a step back.

Clayton's kisses left my cheeks tingling with nerves and excitement. If it weren't for the crickets and loud T.V. coming from inside the house, he probably would have been able to hear how loud my heart was beating in my chest.

"I'll see you tomorrow," he repeated. Except that time it didn't sound like a question.

Clearing my throat, I managed to grin. "Can't wait."

A goofy smile appeared because of that. "Have a goodnight, Lucy."

"You too, Clayton."

I watched as he walked back to his car, my head still spinning with all that had happened that evening.

I didn't get my first kiss, but that was okay because I got something even better: confidence that Clayton Hugh might actually like me as more than just a friend.

Chapter 20

I had almost spent that whole weekend crammed in my room painting. I was so inspired; that Thursday night with Lucy was still replaying in my head again and again. Everything did not go as planned - which was slightly irritating to me - but it turned out to be an amazing evening. She was so understanding, funny, nice...

Everything I already knew she already was, and then some more.

And so my parents had not questioned me locking myself away, only to go out for food and to show them finished pieces. In fact, they probably enjoyed seeing me focus on my old hobby rather than baseball. I do admit, baseball had consumed most of my time once we moved to the states. In Norway, growing up, I spent all of the time sketching, sculpting, and painting. It was my escape from reality that I could not find with anything else. Well, until baseball came into the picture.

My favorite of the weekend thus far was definitely the one I had just finished. It was a painting of Lucy with the color scheme of her favorite color, purple. It wasn't a portrait because it wasn't that realistic, but if anyone knew Lucy, they could recognize it was her immediately.

When I picked up the brush I didn't intend to paint her out. However, the moment I applied the first stroke, the girl who had my mind captured influenced my movements further.

I was about to get up and make my way to far's office, but a knock at my door seized me.

My eyes shot to the clock, and when I realized it was already two-thirty in the afternoon, I cursed softly to myself. I completely lost track of time and forgot Lucy was coming over today.

Trying my best to remain calm, I yelled out, "one second!" Carefully placing the paintings away under my bed, not yet ready to show Lucy my pieces, I wiped my hands on my shorts. Sadly some leftover purple paint smeared onto them.

I gave myself a once over in the mirror. I didn't usually wear my glasses throughout the day, but I was too lazy to put my contacts in. My hair was in need of a cut; my curly hair was starting to show with the unruly spirals poking out to and fro. I tried taming them, but to no avail. I was stuck looking like I had just woken up with the girl I want to impress right outside my door.

"Sorry, sorry." I said aloud as I changed into a clean pair of shorts then spread a little bit of gel through my head.

"I'll wait in the livingroo--" Lucy had started, but she stopped once I swung the door open. Her green eyes were wild with surprise and so many olives and jades. I could stare at them all day and paint them.

"That's not necessary." I stepped back into my room. "My dad's out there anyways. He would ask way too many questions about this sleepwalking stuff." She slowly began to nod her head. I bet she could picture far asking her a billion questions, which was why we tried to keep the conversation to ourselves. "Come on in." I waved her inside.

Lucy walked into my room very cautiously. Her eyes scanned the walls, floor, until finally meeting the bed. She gulped.

"This is the first time you've been back in here since that night, huh?"

She simply nodded, all the while taking in her surroundings more. I was kind of embarrassed - I was in desperate need of having my laundry done. Plus my trash bin was overflowing the slightest bit, but that was okay compared to Zeke's. His trash was full of used condoms.

"It feels like it was so long ago." Lucy finally seemed to fall out of her trance, and held a perky smile. She pulled her long hair to one side, combing through the ends absentmindedly. "But it's been almost three months, I think."

Three months? It felt like I had known Lucy and her parents much longer than that. I could barely even fathom the idea of us being strangers a year before that, yet alone four months previous.

I pulled the bedspread off then flopped down on the mattress. "That's crazy." I shook my head in disbelief, searching for the T.V. remote amongst the blankets. When I found it, I caught a glimpse of Lucy. She was standing on the other side of the bed, blankly staring at the space beside me. "You don't have to be afraid, you know." Her green eyes flashed to me. I smirked. "It's not like it's going to swallow you whole."

"Hardy-har-har." She fake laughed while dramatically rolling her eyes. "I'm just, you know, considering my options. There is a perfectly good chair right there by your desk, after all."

I laid back on the headboard, my lips still curved upright. "But then I wouldn't be beside you. And that's a problem." Yes, I was fully aware my flirting game was switched on. "Plus would you leave me all by my lonesome?" I exasperated, outreaching my hand to her.

If there was one way to make Lucy Walker comfortable, it was by making her laugh. So the moment I saw her pearly teeth once-more I knew she overcame her nerves of the situation.

"Is it safe for me to get in bed with the Clayton Hugh though?" She held her own smirk while crossing her arms. "I've heard some stories, you know. With you and the other girls at school."

My face faltered at that. "Like what?"

"Just things. . . Like, from girls gloating that they've slept with you and stuff." Suddenly the flirtatious mood was simmering down, and Lucy began to pick at her hair once again.

I scoffed. What bullshit. Sure, I hooked up with a few girls and did some things I regretted, but I had never gone that far with someone. I wasn't necessarily waiting out of purity and innocence - more so waiting for the right girl. That was something Mateo followed by too. So of course Zeke had to tease us all the time about still being virgins. At least I never had a scare of having an STD, unlike someone I knew so fondly.

"Well whatever you heard wasn't true. I promise." When I realized I was speaking much more annoyed than intended, I cleared my throat. "I'm not like that. I might have done some dumb things, but not dumb enough to be with girls like that."

Lucy seemed to take in her options one last time, but finally settled for sitting beside me. She got comfortable

"So I actually called my doctor earlier this morning. She specializes in sleeping disorders and used to put me through different trails - medical and physical ones." Lucy began to change the subject, dodging my eyes in the process. As she opened up her phone, I noticed a list of things coming up.

Causes:

- Traumatic event

- Loss of loved one

- Lack of feeling safe

- Stress

"We've already discussed my stress before and I actually do feel a whole lot less stressed out with the yoga I've been doing with my mom."

This should have been a happy thing for her to reveal. Yet there was that cursed frown indented onto her features.

"So obviously my cause of sleepwalking is a lot more deeper than that. And after talking to my dad a bit. . . I think it may have to do with losing my grandpa."

The whole time I had known Lucy, she never once mentioned her grandpa. Of course I had seen pictures at her house of an older man with her while she was younger, but I never questioned who he was. Lucy had explained who everyone else was on the walls but skipped over him. Her eyes would always fall on him, linger there for a second, then move forward to her next relative.

"My grandpa was a good man, you know? I don't even think he got one speeding ticket his whole life. That's just how good my grandpa was." Lucy glanced over at me briefly. Those jade eyes of hers were glazing over, no doubt from the amount of love and grief still churning in her heart for him. "He died when I was eight. A home invasion gone wrong."

She sniffled. Her eyes closed as she faced away from me again. I just wanted to hold her close, but I settled for taking her slender hand in mine.

"During the summer my parents would drop me off at his house in Rhode Island, and we'd do so many things together. He taught me how to ice skate, ride a bike..." She used her free hand to flick a tear away, then chuckled softly to herself. "He even talked to me about boys."

My brows rose at this and I sat up more. "What the heck do you tell an eight year old girl about boys?"

Her laughter continued to be sound to my ears. "He told me how boys had cooties, and that him, my dad, and Jacob should be the only men in my life."

"Me, cooties? Pfft. If anything, you are the one with the cooties." I poked her nose, making her giggle all the more. All I could do was stare at her in that moment of joy in silence. That was until she retreated back to the somber mood she was in before, and made me give her a reassuring hand squeeze. "He sounds amazing, Lucy. Honestly."

To me it sounded like her grandpa was her favorite person way back when. He was an avid drawer, and actually worked as a cartoonist whenever he could; yet managed to be apart of the Major League Baseball League and played for the New York Yankees back in the day. She went on to tell stories of his childhood, and how he went to school with some famous American actress I had no idea about, and how he used to claim they dated briefly.

I sat through it all, truly mesmerized. Not just because Lucy was so in touch with her memories of her grandpa, but because of how much life one man had lived. He sounded so unique and talented - everything I aspired to be.

As the hours passed, and the tears were long gone and smiles were replaced, we somehow ended up cuddling as we began to watch a movie. Her head settled onto my shoulder while her arm made its way across my stomach and my own held her close towards me. I gently pressed my cheek against her hair, the smell of lavender intoxicating me to the point where I couldn't focus on the movie playing.

"Thank you, Clayton." Lucy suddenly whispered out.

I had no clue what she was thanking me for, so I couldn't find a reply.

"I haven't been able to talk about him with anyone for a long time... It felt good. So thank you for listening." She glanced up at me briefly, but enough time for me to see her smile.

Before she moved back to her position, I took the opportunity to kiss her cheek quickly.

"Anytime, love. Anytime..."

And for some reason after all of that, I had a feeling we were one step closer to solving her sleepwalking.

Chapter 21

LUCY

There was one week before the dance. Normally I never thought much about those type of things, but it had been consuming my mind for weeks then. The time was finally nearing and I still had not found the balls to ask Clayton to the dance as my date.

I munched hard on my Fruit Loops, staring even harder at the back of Jacob's big head as he sat on the couch. He was watching some stupid comedy, and his laugh was becoming annoying.

"You sound like a dying cat, ya' know?"

I heard a grunt. "And you sound like a cow chewing its last meal."

"Touché." I shrugged. "But anyways…What are your plans today? Anything dealing with Abby?"

Jacob sighed heavily, as if I were a pestering bug, and paused his movie. He flipped around, a bored expression on his face. "No, she's busy." He looked a little deflated at that, but not enough for me to ask about how their weird not-so-kind-of relationship was going. "We have been texting though."

A brow of mine rose. "About?"

"Clayton."

I groaned. These two couldn't keep out of Clayton and I's business. It was starting to get on my last nerve with Abby, so I told her last week to not say anything else negative about him. Now I don't need to hear the same from my brother.

"Nothing bad, Luce. I promise."

I wanted to believe him, but I knew he wasn't the biggest fan of Clayton. He had never said it, but I could tell by the way he would stare him up in down, trying to size him up whenever they were in the same room. I was pretty sure Clayton was even starting to dislike him then because of that, too.

"Come over here, Lucy. I've been meaning to actually talk about him with you." He didn't sound like his usual amused, sarcastic self. His face even appeared to be caring. It left me daunted in my seat upon the breakfast table. "Oh come on, before I fling my leg at you."

There we go! He sounded and looked like himself again.

I shoved the last bit of cereal in my mouth and then headed over to the couch. He had his prosthetic leg off beside him, while he rubbed the nub of his leg protectively. Pulling the blanket over my body, he stole a piece of it to share with him.

"So, you guys have become good friends since I was last here."

I nodded slowly, my eyes glued to the paused TV screen as if something were playing.

"He treats you well?" Jacob continued.

Yet another nod, but this time is was stronger. Clayton treated me perfectly well. He was a complete gentleman and always wanted me to be as comfortable as possible. I thought Jacob already knew this from the countless other times he had asked me that question, but he obviously wasn't getting the memo or didn't want to believe it.

Jacob was silent for a bit. He ended up continuing the movie, but after a few minutes he turned back to look at me.

"I've never seen you this way about 'just a friend' before."

I had tried my very best to remain calm, but the heat was starting to rise to my cheeks. It suddenly felt a lot hotter than I last remembered.

"How do I appear?"

He hummed for a few moments, and I could tell he was analyzing me. Jacob was very good at reading people, it was one of his many so called "talents". So as I sat there trying my hardest to appear less than effected by our conversation topic of Clayton, I knew he could see through me no matter my attempts.

Clayton had that type of effect on me. Our surprising friendship has escalated into something I couldn't quite put my finger on. Whatever we were, it made me want to smile for hours on end. At least until my cheeks couldn't go any longer.

"You look so. . happy." He blurted out suddenly. Then, he took it back, "--well, besides the fact you aren't smiling. But I can feel how happy you are from the inside out. If that makes any sense at all?" He chuckled nervously. "It reminds me of how I was with someone a while back..."

My brow rose, curious as to who that someone was. He only had a couple of girlfriends throughout the years, and they were all short-lived. At least that is what I had known of.

He must have noticed me catching on to something, because he swiftly turned the subject back to Clayton.

Question after question, Jacob became some sort of therapist trying to get any possible answer out of me. He asked about how Clayton was around his friends, if he was any good at baseball like

I always boasted about. At first it felt weird talking so intimately to Jacob like that, but it grew on me rather quickly. My mind went back to the months I went without seeing him, and how much I should have appreciated times like those with him.

After all, we could have all lost him before.

The ending credits of Jacob's movie began to roll, but he did not seem to mind. We had spent close to an hour just talking about Clayton and I, and it finally appeared like he was done assessing the situation.

"Can I be honest with you, Luce?" He put his hand on my knee, squeezing it a bit.

I expected to hear about how he thought Clayton and I were never going to happen and that I needed to keep my head out of the clouds. So I cleared my throat and shot out, "I already know, I'm getting ahead of myself. But I really do feel like something is there between the two of us. I have never felt so comfortable and happy around a guy before--"

"--Besides with me." He corrected with a sly grin. "And daddy and grandpa." The mention of grandpa made us fall into a small silence, but Jacob continued with what he was going to say before. "Anyways, before I was rudely interrupted. . . I see something special with you and Clayton."

To say I was taken aback was an understatement. This was the guy who could never get his damn name right, yet here he was, further confirming what I was hoping to be true.

"Yeah, sure, I haven't exactly acted like I've liked him, but I definitely do. I mean, have you seen his face?" He fakes a high-pitched giggle. "But in all seriousness; he is a good guy. He makes you happy. What more can a big brother ask for his annoying little sis'?"

I know I had a million ways to react. I could have been overcome with joy that I gave his stinky self a hug, or even be so amused by his "have you seen his face" comment that I could have busted out in laughter. However, for some reason, I ended up shoving him pretty hard on the shoulder.

I wasn't exactly annoyed - I was too happy to be annoyed - but I was definitely feeling a tinge of irritation. All that time I had assumed he hated Clayton, but there he was, saying it was all a facade because he thought it was amusing.

"Well shit, that's not how I thought you'd respond." Jacob eyes squared onto me as if I burned him. "Mooo-om! I just confessed my love for Lucy and Clayton's love and she hurt me!" He yelled out, holding his shoulder like I actually did any damage.

If anything, that was a love tap.

"Yep, I'm the mean one. Definitely," I spoke sarcastically, even with a smile.

We were both playing with each other of course, by my poor mom had no idea about that. She came rushing into the room ready to protect her little boy from my oh-so obvious strength over him.

Her hair was disheveled and her once perfectly crimson lips were now smeared across her chin.

Jacob must have been confused too, because his facade of playing victim fell instantly. Any other day Jacob and I would have assumed something not so kid-friendly went on in their room. However, when our dad appeared out of the hallway scratching his head, we knew something was up.

"I know what you two kids are going to say when I tell you what we just found out, but I just want to clarify something: forty is not too old to have another child, okay? It's the new twenty anyways."

I blinked.

Jacob blinked.

Then, finally, the news she was trying to break finally made it to our slow brains.

"You're pregnant?" Jacob and I both said in unison.

I sounded a lot less excited than him; but that was definitely because if it were true, my youngest child label was going to be stripped.

"Well, after what just happened with us, maybe!" The two not-so adults busted out laughing, pointing at our shocked faces. They revelled in our twitching brows and disgusted expressions.

Sometimes I wondered who were the kids in this family, because I definitely couldn't be the baby of it.

"We're not pregnant." My mom wiped a fake tear away, then clasped her hands together. "Thank goodness. But a family we know are expecting a baby now..."

Jacob and I sat there, waiting for them to say who was expecting. I was thinking it might have been the Anderson's across the street. They are always popping kids out, so that wouldn't be too surprising.

"Looks like Clayton isn't going to be an only child anymore, Lucy. You're gonna have a sister-in-law!"

I didn't know what to be more surprised over: the fact my mom thought Clayton and I were gonna make it down the aisle, or there was gonna be another cute Hugh addition to the world.

It was honestly good news to me, because I loved babies and children in general. The only thing that worried me was that Clayton hadn't told me.

"Before you get mad at your boyfriend..." My dad chimed in from behind my mom, beginning to wave a finger at me. "-- which I can tell you are starting to. He doesn't know yet. And you can't tell him yet."

Oh, shit. They knew how bad I was at keeping secrets from people. Especially people I was close to.

"Tomorrow they want to get some people together at their house for a barbeque, and they are going to break the news then. So don't worry Lucy, you don't have to keep it from him for too long."

I breathed out a little bit. I was always bad at keeping secrets. Maybe it was because I felt insanely guilty keeping things from certain people, I wasn't too sure. But if I had to keep a monumental secret like this one, I would no matter what.

I'd just suffer in the process.

After that little revelation, I ended up heading to my room to lay around. Clayton was busy that day helping Mateo with his baseball, so I was not so patiently waiting for them to finish so we could text. I tried working on some homework, but I was too distracted on the idea of Clayton with a baby.

That would be so cute...

The ring of my phone almost shook the pencil out of my hand. I was expecting a text from Clayton, but I got something even better: a phone call.

"Hey, Clay." I smiled into the phone. "How did the practice go?"

He sounded like he was moving some things around. "It went alright, he still has a long way to go." There was some more shuffling on the other end of the line. "But anyways, I was wondering if you wanted to come to my house tomorrow? My parents are throwing some random barbeque, and they expect me to get the whole house ready for company by then."

I chuckled a little bit. "Are you asking me to come to the barbeque or save you from cleaning your whole house?"

"Well let's just say if you come a little earlier you'll be treated to some milkshakes and tater tots." I could almost imagine the inevitable smirk on his face.

As long as he were there working alongside me, I didn't need any kind of bribe to urge me to help out. The shakes and tots were just a triple bonus.

"Of course I'll help. How about I come at noon?"

I could hear a car door shut. "Yeah, that works. Thank you so much, Lucy. You're the best."

"I know." I fell back on my bed, grabbing my stuffed elephant to hug tight to my chest. Clayton's laugh had that effect on people.

"Well, I should probably let you go now. I'm gonna drive over to town and grab some things from the store for tomorrow. I'll let you know when I get home."

"Oh, okay! Drive safe. Love you."

The minute the words fell out of my mouth, I regretted it. It came out so naturally because normally I said good-bye to my parents like that. It was a mistake that made me freeze in my spot, eyes clamped shut with fear.

"Uh, yeah. I will Lucy. Bye.."

I wasn't sure what scared me the most: the fact I accidently said I love you to a guy I might have actually fallen for, or that he seemed just as freaked out by it as I was.

Way to go, Walker. Way to go.

Chapter 22

Love was a word I rarely ever used. My parents never showered me with the constant use of the word as I grew up. Did I think that was a bad thing? No, quite the opposite actually. It made the word, the actually feeling, a lot more special to all of us whenever we said it to one another.

When Lucy made that obvious slip up while ending our call, it had caught me off guard. I knew it was a mistake the minute it came out, but it led me to thinking about the word way more than I would have liked.

What did actual romantic love feel like? How would I know I'm actually in love with someone?

I was sure most guys went to their buddies for their past experiences in the love department, but of course my friends never even saw the word as a possibility. Zeke would laugh at my face for hours on end if I ever mentioned that I was interested in such a feeling - yet alone might actually feel such a thing for someone.

It had started to nag the back of my mind the rest of that day. I tried my best to focus on helping my parents prepare for the barbeque the next day, but it was difficult for me. Besides my predicament, the two of them were behaving strangely as of a week before.

They weren't the type of people to randomly throw a party, especially one so last minute and not falling on a holiday.

I wanted to bring my suspicions that something was up with Lucy, and since I was nearby on yet another grocery run, I decided to stop by her house.

I would have let her know I was coming, but I knew she would have avoided me because of her little mess up from before. That little visit was going to help me show her it was okay, and that it happens. I definitely did that a lot when it came to my teachers and accidently calling them mor or far. It was embarrassing, but shit happens.

My hands grew slightly damp as I trudged up the stairs, their red door staring me down.

I had never told Lucy that a couple years previous, when I had first became friends with my baseball pals, that we teepeed her house. Well, they did mostly… but I watched, even laughed a little.

The next day was when I first noticed Lucy Walker, but because of all the wrong reasons. She sat next to me for weeks without grabbing my attention, until I overheard her explaining to her friends her house was teepeed. That was the moment where I saw what my behavior was doing to others, not just myself. I began to analyze Zeke and how he acted. The cool, popular image I once saw of him was shattered by the look on Lucy's face.

From then on, I always noticed when Lucy was in a class with me, or if she passed me in the hallway, or sat by my table in the cafeteria. She was beyond cute I thought, but never believed I was good enough to go right up to her and ask her out.

Yet here I was, growing closer and closer to this girl I used to be fixated on from afar. . . All because she quite literally walked into my life.

As my hand reached up to knock on the door, this feeling I couldn't quite depict began to consume me. It left the tips of my fingers tingly and chest full.

"Who is it?" I could hear Jacob yell out. He sounded annoyed, which was just plain perfect. Queue being called the wrong name in three. . two. . "Oh, hey, Clayton." He swung the door open, perplexed to see me there.

It was nearing nine-thirty, which was pretty late, so I didn't blame him for the surprise.

"You called me Clayton?" I was dumbfounded. Had he called me the correct name before? If he had, I couldn't remember a time.

He rubbed his eyes for a moment, then a smirk appeared slowly but surely. "That is your name isn't it?"

I stepped inside once he let me in, and I was greeted by Mr. and Mrs. Walker sitting in the livingroom.

Mr. Walker raised an eyebrow. "Don't you think it's pretty late to be visiting my daughter, sir?"

He was a very confusing individual to me. Mr. Walker could go from a fellow pal to a guy ready to pull out his shotgun on me. It was understandable since he was protecting his daughter, but definitely scared me shitless on the occasion.

"Uhh--"

"I invited him over to hang out with me for a bit, chill yourself." Jacob came swooping in to my rescue. "We'll be in the game room."

"But I--"

"Shush if you want to see her," he whispered over his shoulder at me.

I listened without missing a beat. Mr. Walker didn't really question us after that, and Mrs. Walker offered me some snacks to take with us.

We started to make our way down the hallway, and when we stopped by Lucy's room, I noticed her door was shut and light turned off. Well, I guess that was why she had not texted me back yet. She must've fallen asleep while watching Archer.

I reached my hand out to knock, but Jacob stopped me. He waved me over to follow him, so I obliged in fear he would hurt me otherwise.

"Welcome to my man cave. The place where Lucy avoids at all costs, which is great for me, because that means nothing of mine is moved out of place." He opened the door to a room I had never been in before, and I almost wanted to get sort of mad at Lucy for not telling me about this before. The room was full of movies and videogames, a screen projector hanging on one side of the room, while the main wall had two flat screens with counsels under them. "Please don't change the order of the DVD's and games. They are in order of release, and are my preciouses."

When Lucy told me Jacob was organized, I had no clue he was this organized. I barely had one folder for school to throw all my work together. That was my version of organized.

"Wow..." That's all I could muster out.

Jacob chuckled a bit to himself while settling into a bean bag in the corner. When he gestured towards the one beside him, I assumed that was for me.

Not so gracefully I maneuvered around the coffee table, trying to overlook the intense stare Jacob was sending me.

"So, I'm sure you're wondering why I saved you from getting kicked out just a bit ago, huh?"

I nodded. "Yeah. Strangely uncharacteristic of you."

Jacob put his hands up. "Hey now. I'm a pretty chill dude as long as you don't screw up my strategic placement of items and not hurt my little sister."

I gulped at the last part. What if Lucy found my nervous farewell after saying love you to me as a bad thing and got hurt?

"Don't worry, bud." He patted my knee with just two fingers, his face contorted for a moment with disgust. Then he continued, "you haven't hurt my sister." I eased up at that. "Not yet, at least."

"I don't plan on it," I surprisingly declared, without missing a bit. This made Jacob nod his head.

"So, what's your relationship with my sister exactly?"

It was a question so many people had started to ask me. Even my past fling Courtney was asking what was going on between Lucy and I. I used to tell them we were just friends, but now when people ask, I wasn't too sure how to answer. I wanted to be so much more than friends, but I was too scared of rejection to take that leap without confirmation of her feeling the same way.

"You like her, don't you?" He asked, his face growing soft for once.

"Of course I like her she's great--"

"No. You like her as more than just a friend." It didn't sound like he was asking if I did or not. He was more so stating a fact he believed in. One that was one-hundred percent true. "Don't play dumb with me either Clayton Hugs."

"It's, uh, Hugh. Clayton Hugh." I added gently.

"Shit, man. I'm sorry." He rubbed the back of his head. "I'm really trying."

"It's alright. You can memorize all these release dates, but not my name. Totally get it."

The air was lightened with our mutual laughter.

"I'm not going to lie to you, Clayton. When I first saw you, I just saw this boy trying to get into my sister's pants." He pointed at my face. "I mean look at you. You kind of scream heartthrob... but anyways, you have proven me otherwise."

I didn't know what to say or do, so I sat back and listened. This was the first actual conversation he and I was sharing, and it wasn't the worst experience of my life, that was for sure.

"But you know what you are?"

I leaned forward, truly curious. "Huh?"

"Stupid as hell."

And, there went the nice conversation we were having.

"No offense dude, but why haven't you told Lucy how you feel? You two look so happy when you are hanging out." Jacob looked away from me to turn the T.V. on, making my gaping expression less embarrassing for myself. "What's stopping you?"

For so long I was keeping all my feelings bottled up on the inside. The only person who actually knew how I felt about Lucy was Mateo, and he definitely did not hear all the details, and just about how much I actually felt for this girl.

"Lucy's too good for me. She can find someone a lot better."

Jacob started to mess with his prosthetic leg, his eyes tracing up and down it. "You know, I used to think this one girl was too good for me too. I thought she deserved someone who had both two feet on the ground.. Literally and metaphorically." When he glanced up at me, regret was planted on his face. "I lost my shot with her, and now she's about to marry a big shot Hollywood producer."

"Oh... I'm sorry."

He waved me off. "But, uh, enough of me. Back to you. I'm telling you from experience that sitting back and letting something amazing slip out of your fingers because of your insecurities sucks absolute balls." He had to pause for a moment to keep himself calm.

"Yes, I know.. but I really don't know if she feels the same way as I do."

He snorted out loud - loud enough to where I wouldn't be surprised if Lucy woke up because of it.

"Once again dude, you're not the brightest when it comes to Lucy. She has been crazy about you since day one. I'm pretty sure even before day one." He faked like he was curling his nonexistent long hair. "Mom, isn't he the cutest guy you've ever seen? Oh my goodness. He's sooo totes dreamy."

Despite his over dramatic, nasally interpretation of Lucy, all I could do was smile. My face fell into my hands as I blew out a long breath. It felt like I was holding that one in for the longest time.

"Now just because she likes you does not mean you can park your car in her garage. Remember what we talked about before? That still remains." He tugged at my hair a bit to make me look at him.

I knew it wasn't the response he was looking for, but that smile was still remaining. How could I frown at a moment like that? The idea of Lucy liking me since the beginning made me beyond surprised and ecstatic; all while feeling stupid too, of course.

"I understand. I haven't even thought about that."

"Are you forgetting I am a fellow male?" He gave me a straight, dull face. "You don't have to act like you haven't thought about it."

Okay, maybe I had. . . on occasions. I would have never told him that though. Then my car would have definitely gotten crushed.

Before I had a chance to say anything or change the subject, a loud alarm noise sounded off from a speaker in the corner of the room. It made me physically shake and I was quick to hop up.

Jacob appeared used to it. All he did was sigh. "It's just Lucy. She must have gotten out of her bed."

"Does that happen when she has to go to the bathroom at night, too?" I followed him out the door and down the hallway. Lucy's parents were already making their way to her bedroom but they backed away once they saw we had it taken care of.

"No, she can put the password in to turn it off on her phone." He answered smoothly while fiddling with her doorknob.

Lucy told me a little about how they somehow locked her in her room at night majority of the time. However, it was more of just a baby lock where she could easily get out if she was actually awake. It was a lot less horrifying as it had sounded.

Jacob opened the door slowly to peek inside, then eventually opened it fully.

"Just making sure she has clothes on tonight."

My brows rose at that. Was he saying she slept naked sometimes?

"Stop thinking of her naked now, boy."

I stepped inside her room behind him with burnt cheeks, to find Lucy there, standing eerily across from us. She was wearing cute polka dot pajama pants and a tank top that had ventured a little low. Her eyes, however, were the main focus though.

Her eyes remained open and vacant.

"It's not good to wake up anyone from sleepwalking, but I'm sure you know this already." Jacob whispered as he neared Lucy. "The alarm only goes off if she moves pretty far from her bed. See?" He pointed to the sensors attached to the bottom of her walls. "Sometimes she doesn't make it this far every night. She must've been stressed about something."

I could make out faint murmuring coming from Lucy, making me move closer to her. I just wanted to hold her.

"Anyways, the alarm only sounds in the other rooms of the house, so she isn't woken up by it. Then whenever one of us comes in here, we try to gently put her back in bed." He continued to explained. It was hard to pay attention when I had Lucy staring back at me so squarely. "This time around, you're gonna be the person to get her back in bed."

I definitely paid attention to what he had said then.

"What? No, I don't want to hurt her," I instantly retracted, taking a few steps away from her. The last thing I wanted to do was make things worse for her. I couldn't imagine having to go through these measures every night.

Jacob shook his head. "It's not as bad as you think. Promise."

Lucy started to take a step forward getting closer to running into her dresser. I move forward instantly, gently gripping her arms.

"Now, just slowly guide her over to her bed. She will typically move herself with you, unless she's being stubborn. . then I typically just pick her up and throw her over there."

My eyes shot to him.

"Kidding, kidding."

Slowly I began to move her closer to her bed, all the while holding her little by little closer to myself. Ignoring the fact she was deadpanning me, she looked so peaceful. How could she ever even fall asleep not knowing if she'll get up and accidently hurt herself somehow?

My mind fell back to the night we first officially met. She escaped the house and made it to my house! It was such a miracle for her to make it out without a scratch. The idea of anything happening to her made me want to hold her tight to my chest and never let her go.

"I got the rest of it, thanks, Clayton." Jacob stepped in to get Lucy to lay back down in her bed.

She settled back in pretty much on her own, which was strange to me. Jacob said that somehow she would recognized the softness, and automatically assume it's her bed.

"I'm gonna go let my parents know it's all good. Close the door when you leave." I nodded towards Jacob, then peered down at Lucy.

Her eyes had closed when I wasn't looking and she was beginning to mumble actual words out.

As beautiful as she was, all I could think about was how horrible her issue was. I wanted to help fix her problem so she could have at least one night of good sleep. I wanted to help her so much.

"Don't worry, love. We'll figure this out."

There was a piece of her blanket not covering her arm, so I gingerly placed it over her more.

With one last glance over her, I bent down to kiss her cheek.

I went to leave her room after that, pleased with getting more insight in her condition and nightly routine, when I heard her mumble something before I made it out.

"You're so perfect, Clay.."

My head whipped around, to find Lucy snuggling up more into her bed and blanket, a small smile gracing her face. Despite her being asleep, my cheeks still heated up.

"...Søte drømmer (Sweet dreams)."

Chapter 23

My brother was one of those types of people who heard the word "clean" and didn't stick their bottom lip out. In fact, when I told Jacob that next day I was going to help Clayton with his cleaning duties, he cracked a huge smile. He even tagged along with me to speed up the process.

However since Clayton only bribed me with milkshakes and tater-tots, there was none waiting at Clayton's house for Jacob.

Jacob, being the bitter guy he was, decided we didn't need his help any further. He made himself comfortable on the couch.

We didn't need him though. It didn't take too long, and to my surprise, it was a whole lot of fun.

The Hugh family as a whole was super bright and bubbly. I could see where Clayton got his likability from. And to think there was going to be another on the way.

"I still don't understand why we're doing all of this?" Clayton questioned out of the blue to his parents in the livingroom. I was wiping down their kitchen counters, so I peeked out into the room. "This seems like a bit much."

"We just thought it would be fun. We haven't seen some people for a long time." Mrs. Hugh explained pretty eloquently if I say so myself.

"Plus I just want to party." Mr. Hugh chimed in with a sly grin.

Thankfully Clayton shrugged it off and didn't question anymore after that.

Five o'clock was about to be around the corner, and we managed to make everything look great. Jacob, being the lazy boy he was, had fallen asleep on the living room couch stage; even through the vacuuming stage. So, of course, Clayton had to mess with him.

He took a feather from one of his pillows that had a hole in it, and began tickling the tip of Jacob's nose. When that wouldn't startle him awake, and it stopped being funny, I straight up smacked him on the forehead and then ran off into the kitchen.

"What the hell?" Jacob mumbled. "Clayton?"

I could tell Clayton was receiving a deadly look from Jacob because he looked scared as could be.

My laughter couldn't be contained any longer, and I didn't want Clayton to get bitch slapped by my brother, so I let it out. Sure, Jacob got pissy with me, but it was worth it one-hundred-percent.

"You almost got your boyfriend killed, Luce." Jacob smirked at me, finally seeing the humor in the situation.

However, his humor was different than mine. His comment made me stop laughing and become a bright red.

"Oh, come on. I'm kidding. No need to get all blushy and weird." Jacob chuckled, wiping the grogginess out of his eyes.

That last hour was pretty much us messing with one another. It was a different kind of messing with each other though. It was friendly, and light hearted. When Jacob made comments towards

Clayton now, it didn't seem hostile anymore. They were actually getting along really well, and I loved every bit of it.

Soon enough, one by one people began to come into the Hugh household. It wasn't a huge turnout, still holding a very intimate feeling. Despite that, I was still very nervous. I always got that way around people, even if I looked my best. It didn't help that Clayton was away socializing with his guests - some he had not seen in a long, long time.

There was another girl who had just arrived, and he was with her in the kitchen while she hugged Clayton's parents. There squeals of happiness whenever she entered the house. I didn't really know who she was, but she was very pretty. She almost looked like the female version of Clayton, if that could have been possible. But whoever she was, she seemed really important to the Hugh family.

Her bright eyes scanned back out into the livingroom where I sat with my brother and strangers, and they locked on me. Instantly my eyes jumped to the closest object, but that did not help.

I could hear Clayton tell the girl no a bunch of times, sounding fairly flustered. Then he spurred out a bunch of words in his native tongue, leaving me all the more confused.

The girl raced towards me with a beautiful smile. "You must be Lucy!"

She was beaming, even under the subpar lighting of the over-head fan.

"Uh... hi." My hands squeezed the bottom of my skirt.

Before she could say another word, Clayton stepped in with a pointed look towards her. "This is my good, good friend Greta. I've known her since we were kids."

I had never heard about Greta before from him. My jaw clenched slightly.

"Oh, cool. It's nice to meet you." I finally said to Greta, her eyes still beaming.

It looked like she was about to talk to me some more, but thankfully Mrs. Hugh whisked her away to the kitchen. She left behind a pretty winded looking Clayton, and me slightly…jealous. I had never felt so jealous before that moment. Sure, I would get slightly irritated at the thought of Clayton and his old fling Courtney together, but I never thought too much into it.

That girl was different to him though. I could see their connection from a mile away and that pulled the corner of my lips down. And I wasn't afraid for Clayton to see my frown, too.

He peeked over his shoulder, stealing a look at his good friend in the kitchen, and then sat next to me.

There were a couple people sitting nearby, so he leaned over near my ear.

"I've told her all about you." His warm breath on my neck nearly made me shake. "And I promise you have nothing to worry about."

Despite him being so close, I couldn't help but turn my face towards him.

He was merely inches away from me, yet I couldn't decipher his expression. All I could do was marvel at his twinkling eyes, forgetting that we were at a party. I honestly could have stayed in that position for hours on end.

All good things must come to end though, and that moment was no exception. Our dads stormed back into the house and announced they finished the cooking. They had set up the food on tables in the back, and once again Clayton and I parted our ways.

Jacob kept me company while everyone ate after failing to sweet talk Greta.

"I don't get why girls don't like me. I," he shoved mashed potatoes in his mouth then smiled, "--am a true catch."

He did manage to get a chuckle out of me, but I swatted at his knee. "Quit being gross, dude."

"That's my middle name though?"

I rolled my eyes. "How original."

"Shut up, shut up. She's comin' this way." Jacob was the one to swat my knee that time.

I looked up from my plate and sure enough, Greta was striding up to us. What Clayton had told me earlier definitely made me feel better, but come on. Staring at this model-like girl left me feeling intimidated. I couldn't help but feel slightly bitter.

"Hey Lucy... and, uh, Lucy's brother." Greta gave a short smile to Jacob. I would have too; he had a little bit of BBQ sauce across his chin. "I just wanted to thank you for being such a good friend to Clayton. I know he's had a hard time adjusting here. And ever since he's met you, he has looked and sounded happier than ever." She chuckled. "He used to have such bad taste in girls.. but you? I can tell you're a good one."

Leave it up to me and my inability to talk at the worst of times. I sat there gaping up at her, wanting to speak, but I couldn't. It all got caught in my throat.

She didn't miss a beat though. "I hope while I'm here for the next couple days we can hang out? Yeah?"

I nodded. Then nodded. And of course, kept nodding like a loser.

"Great. Well, I'll see you later."

Usually with girls that looked like Greta, if I ever had a bad case of shyness, I would've been looked at like I was crazy. Kind of like how Jacob was reacting to me when Greta walked off. I could feel his judgement. But her? I could tell she was a genuine, happy person. She definitely wasn't a threat.

"Okay everyone, everyone!" Mr. Hugh stood on one of the picnic table benches. "I know everyone is slightly confused as to why we pulled this little get together out of nowhere."

My eyes brightened. They were finally going to announce the great news! It was so hard for me not to spill the beans to Clayton about him finally being an older brother, but now that it was finally about to happen, I needed to find him.

He was across the backyard around some of his dad's cousins, so I quickly scurried over there and sat by him. I was welcomed with a smile.

"This is kind of weird." He whispered to me. "They normally don't make a speech at these sort of things."

All I could do was shrug.

"As some of you may know, our family of three has always been the light of our lives." Mrs. Hugh said. The two parents looked towards each other. "Of course, for many years we did try to make it four, but we ended up not fighting fate after so long. If we were meant to be three, then that's how it was supposed to be."

I glimpsed over at Clayton, and he looked so confused and cute.

"But... it seems like fate had other plans for us."

There were gasps. There were squeals. Pretty sure one of the squeals was from Jacob, even though he already knew the big news like the dweeb he was.

I mostly kept my focus on Clayton though. To see the different emotions crossing through his face was a beautiful sight.

"We're expecting!" The two finally yelled out together, hand in hand.

There was an eruption of claps and cheers. People were standing up and going up to the expected parents for hugs and congratulations.

Clayton's reaction was the best to me though. It was so sweet and simple, that it made my toes curl in my shoes.

He looked over at me, mouth slightly open. "Wait.. so I'm going to be a big brother?"

I placed my hand over his, and squeezed it. "And you're going to be the best big brother, ever!"

Clayton's eyes softened at that. Then, like a switch, he went into celebratory mode. He hopped up, ran over to his parents and grabbed them both in an enormous hug.

The rest of the night was an absolute blast. Although I didn't see Clayton the majority of the night after the reveal, I still had a lot of fun.

I finally had gotten over my shyness with Greta, and we talked a good amount. She told me about her boyfriend of three years, and how she used to want to marry Clayton when she was ten but Clayton never wanted anything to do with her. She told me some juicy stories about pre-cool Clayton, and how much of a cute dork he was.

We probably would have kept on talking, but J.K. had finally showed up. She was late because her parents had grounded her, and she was looking for the perfect opportunity to sneak out. I warned her against it, but ever since she got tangled with that toxic boy Zeke, I've seen the goodie-goodie go a little bad.

"Wait, so y'all aren't going to the dance together?"

Jacklyn Kate's question was kind of deflating to my fun evening. It was tough to wrap my head over, but no, Clayton and I weren't going to the dance together. At least not as dates. However, I am very determined to dance with him at least once, or maybe more.

"..no, but before you preach about how I need to--"

"Hey, ladies!" My mom knocked on the guest room door, where we had tucked ourselves away from everyone else for a reason. "What are y'all doing cooped up in here when a bunch of cute guys arrived a while ago?"

I wanted to gag a little bit. "Ma, those guys are way too young for you to be saying that. Plus aren't that cute, either."

"Hey, that's what you think." J.K. turned to my mom with a wicked smile. "The tall dark and mysterious one is mine currently." She winked.

My mom laughed at that, and even I did for a bit, but I still didn't like that Zeke guy. J.K. could do so much better, and she has in the past. He had douche written all over him. She just wouldn't hear any of my protests anymore. Even after he kind of ghosted her.

"Well, I'll leave you guys here then. I was actually asked by a special someone where my daughter was, so I'll just let him know you don't want to see him. ." My mom hummed a little, slowly making her way back to the door.

It didn't take a rocket scientist for me to figure out who was asking about me. Instantly I shot up and gave J.K. a mock salute. She would have done the same thing if she heard Zeke was asking for her.

My mom rolled her eyes at me, but I did not care.

"He said he was going to his room to get something to show you." She added while I was heading in the wrong direction.

I turned around not so smoothly, earning a few looks from the strangers at the party, and headed towards the direction of his room. His door was shut, which made my steps slower.

Gulping, I reached up and knocked on the door. Maybe he wanted to show me some information he found that could help my sleepwalking? Or maybe he wanted to show me an art piece he finished for school that he was pretty proud of.

There was a feint "come in" from behind the door, but I still cautiously opened the door. When I didn't see him anywhere in his room, I was confused. Then he walked out of his closet and I jumped a little bit.

"Sorry, sorry." He held his hands up. "I was just wondering if you could help a guy out?"

He held up two ties, all the while looking absolutely amazing in a black and white suit. If I hadn't known him already, I would have thought he was a celebrity or bigshot athlete. That's how yummy he was looking.

"Wha-at?" I blinked.

Clayton let out a breathy laugh. "This is embarrassing, but I was hoping you could help me chose a tie and teach me how to tie one for the dance next week."

Once I got back to my senses, I finally shut the door behind me. "You decided to do this right in the middle of the party?" I mused.

He shrugged. "Sometimes it can be a bit overwhelming and you just want to get away."

I looked him up and down, without any filter, and once I caught what I was doing I turned away from him. I didn't want him to see the blush on my cheeks.

"The second tie would go great with the suit." I commented, still heated in the cheeks.

Clayton took a couple steps near me, startling me to look up at him. He was getting so darn close. Sometimes I had wished he didn't have such an effect on me. I just wanted to act normal in front of him.

I watched as he placed tie number one on his dresser, then placed each end of tie number two in each hand. He gave me this sort of devilish smile. One that if I wasn't mistaken, was definitely on the more flirtier side. He then proceeded to place the tie around my head, as if he were about to put it on me, except instead of tying it, he softly tugged me a step closer to him. I could smell the slightest bit of alcohol on his breath.

It was a playful gesture made by him, probably meant to be light hearted, but my breath got caught.

He must've felt the change in atmosphere too, because his smile faded. Suddenly I felt like we were back on my porch, with the crickets sounding around us; that feeling that maybe I'd finally have my first kiss resurfacing.

"Do.. do you still need me to do your tie?" I gulped.

There was a quick flick of his tongue across his lips. I couldn't help but look at them.

"Oh." He chuckled, dropped the tie from around my head. He took a step back and handed it to me.

Settling my breathing, my poor hands were not as easy to control. I grabbed the tie, but my hands visibly shook as I began going step by step on Clayton how to tie it.

"It's actually really simple with practice. As long as you're smarter than Jacob, that is. He's the reason why I know how to." I patted his chest once I finished it. He looked so handsome.

Clayton looked away from me finally, and to his mirror. He nodded his head and cracked another grin. "Thanks, Lucy. I know who to call next Friday if I need help getting ready."

I knew he meant that as a sweet comment, but it made me slightly sad. I wanted to be the girl he was getting ready for to go to the dance with.

"Definitely."

Eventually we had to go back out into the party, before people questioned where we were and what we were doing. My dad was already starting to get ideas but my mom had to keep assuring him we weren't doing anything scandalous.

The party was finally coming to an end, and majority of the family and friends had left already. It was my family's time next to leave, so I went up to the happy expecting parents and gave each of them a hug.

"I hope you enjoyed yourself tonight, Lucy. Thanks for all of your help today." Mrs. Hugh hugged me tight. "You know if you ever feel in the cleaning mood, feel free to come over here!" We laughed. "And not to be nosey, but what were you and Clayton doing in his room for so long earlier? Was he alright?"

"Oh, yeah. He was very happy, actually." I could tell his parents were worried that Clayton wouldn't be as accepting to the news, but he loved the idea of being a big brother. "I was just teaching him how to do his tie for the dance next week."

The two looked at each other, and then gave me a confused expression. "Wait, you were teaching him how to?"

"Uh, yeah. Why?"

Mr. Hugh chuckled, shaking his head. "That boy is trying to work his magic, momma." He turned to his wife and wrapped his arm around her. "It's what the Hugh boy's are known for."

"I don't follow." I was starting to feel super awkward.

Mrs. Hugh gave her husband a pointed look, then a soft smile towards me. "Clayton is quite the master to tying a tie, actually. But anyways, if you don't go out there to the car, I think your parents may leave you."

I wasn't fully able to register that, but I said a quick good-bye and headed out the door. She was right, my dad was already backed out into the road and ready to zip off into the moonlight.

I hopped into the car as fast as I could, but before we drove off, I glimpsed back towards Clayton's bedroom window. His lights were turned off, and he was probably knocked out.

What a sneaky little flirt Clayton Hugh could be... Who knew?

Chapter 24

C LAYTON

If someone two months ago would have told me I would've been taking the dance so seriously, I would have laughed at them right in the face. It wasn't because I didn't enjoy a good party, because I definitely did on occasion, but this dance was different. It made me feel nervous.

The first year I had moved to Ridgewood, it was pretty close to the fall dance. I barely knew anyone. Zeke and Mateo only gave me glances in classes, and I had no idea how to approach them, yet alone girls to ask to the dance.

For some reason though, out of the blue, I had caught the interest of a senior girl. When word around the school went that she asked me to the dance, Zeke and Mateo swooped in on me. Zeke claimed he had chosen to take me under his wing, but Mateo later told me he just didn't want me taking that girl off the market.

So, being the naive guy I was, I listened to Zeke when he had told me I was better off rejecting her offer and not going to the "lame" dance. Ever.

Fast forward three years, and there I was doing my tie before Lucy's parents dropped her off at my house.

Sighing at the mirror, I tried to tame a curl that was fighting against the load of hairspray my mom sprayed.

"Hey there handsome," my mom knocked on the door, peeking her head in. "Mrs. Walker just let me know they are about to head here. I'm about to leave for work, too. So you should come out here."

I wanted to move and listen to her right away, but for some reason my feet were stuck to the ground.

"You're nervous, huh, baby?" She cooed, coming to my side at once. There was a soft smile gracing her face. "It's okay to admit that."

I could only chuckle out awkwardly. "Nervous? About what?"

She flicked her eyes around. "Okay, if you don't want to say it you don't have to. But she feels the same way. I promise you, bud." She grabbed my hand and gave it a nice, reassuring squeeze. Something I needed way too much.

"Have I ever told you I love you?" This time, my nerves weren't so evident in my laughter.

We walked into the living room in just the knick of time. I could see headlights flash through the blinds.

Lucy's parents decided to drop her off at my house since her dad needed to do some tinkering under the hood of her car apparently. So I was going to drive us to the school, and for what I understood, she was spending the night at J.K.'s house later that evening.

So it wasn't like we were showing up as a couple.

Or maybe it could be like that? I was starting to not give a damn anymore.

"Open doors for her, ask her if she wants something to drink when y'all get there. Try not to step on her toes if you two end up dancing. Also, remember to--"

"Momma," I said slowly, trying to calm her down.

I used to call my parents momma and pappa all the time before we moved here, but I had started to call them mor and far as a way to feel more connected to our culture. It was the formal version, sure, but neither minded.

"You act like I haven't taken a girl out before."

She scoffed. "Not one like this. The others were all skank--"

There was a couple knocks at the door, making my mom shut up. When neither of them moved towards the door, I sighed, and trudged over to let Lucy in.

You want to know what Eleanora Whitman, the senior that asked me three years ago to the dance, wore? She wore a tight, short black dress with a very deep-V; it fit her personality perfectly. It just happened to be a style and personality I wasn't a huge fan of.

Lucy, though...

She was wearing a maroon dress that hugged her waist then fell loose over her thighs. It wasn't too short nor long, but I could still see her holding it down further. Her hair was pulled back besides a couple curls around her face, and around her neck glimmered a sparkly necklace.

She looked gorgeous.

"Oh," Lucy suddenly said. "Thanks, Clay. You look pretty nice yourself."

I said that out loud? Abort, abort.

"No problem." I tried to say as calmly as possible.

Meanwhile our parents were watching us with weird smiles. They insisted we take about a thousand photos together until they let us leave. It wasn't as nerve wracking as I had previously thought as I had wrapped my arm around her waist, pulled her close, and said cheese to the camera. If anything, it felt natural.

Before they were done taking pictures, I snuck a small kiss on the cheek in there. I'm pretty sure her eyes turned out wide and big in the picture, but that was okay. Our parents loved it. I did too.

I was hoping the rest of the evening would go just as smoothly.

I was surprised to see Zeke pull into the parking lot. Last time I checked, these sort of things were lame. Then again, he does have something going on with J.K., so maybe he was finally turning around his douchebag ways.

Trying to not pay too much attention to him, I turned towards Lucy. My fingers reached out to hers, as I guided her around a group of people who decided the best place to talk was right in front of the doors.

"Tonight is going to be a lot of fun." I flashed her a smile. "I can feel it."

"Yeah, me too." She nodded.

As we walked in, I was actually quite impressed by how much they transformed our plain gym. The room glowed a dark blue, our school colors, and had a stage set up with a band playing. Tables were lined up, each one having different types of foods and beverages. We were greeted by the assistant principal, which gestured us to sign our names on the entry list next to our own.

"Did you want me to get you something to drink?" I asked. In the back of my head, I saw mor with a proud smile.

Lucy peeked over at me. "Uh, sure." She fiddled with her thumbs. "I'll take some root beer."

I left Lucy where she was, hurrying to the refreshment table. From the corner of my eye I could see her look around, obviously uncomfortable. If only she knew she was the prettiest girl there that night, she would have had nothing to worry about.

It didn't take me too long to get the drinks. If it wasn't for Mr. Wharton, one of my past teachers, I would have been back to Lucy in a blink of an eye. But of course he wanted to catch up, asked if I thought about playing ball in college -- and do not get me started on how interested he was in what colleges I was thinking about already.

"You know, it is really smart to apply early around this time. You could probably make it into a nice school in the city, if you really tried to." He continued on.

I nodded my head, finally turning around to see if Lucy was still doing okay.

Except that time she wasn't there.

"I'll see you later, Mr. Wharton. . ." He was still going on about something, but I was already walking away.

I knew Lucy was her own person and could venture off with friends, but that was the thing. I was looking at her group of friends across the gym and she was nowhere in sight with them. I could feel something was off.

"Hey, Abby. Have you seen where Lucy is?"

I knew I was the last person she was wanting to talk to here by the roll of her eyes. "Not even together yet and you're this controlling?"

Sighing, I moved on to J.K. "Did you see where she went?"

J.K. brows furrowed deeply. "I was actually wondering where Zeke went too."

Then it clicked.

I saw the way he was looking at her when we had first arrived. Plus there was no way he had come there to the dance not to stir up some kind of trouble; whether it be with J.K., or my relationship with Lucy.

I left the girls and trudged through the gym doors, where low and behold, Lucy and Zeke were.

Neither of them could see me, since they were tucked away between cars.

"Look, I'm sorry for dragging you out here, but I had to be the one to tell you." The closer I walked towards them, the clearer Zeke's words got. "But Clayton has been playing you."

My brows rose. How could he say that? He knew how much I felt for Lucy, and there he was lying to her about them. Grinding my teeth, I clenched my fists tight. Zeke must have been too engrossed in his bullshit lie, that he didn't hear me walking up behind him. Lucy did though, and her watery eyes connected with mine.

"You didn't actually think a guy like him would like a girl like you, right? He thinks he's way out of your league."

It was starting to get to the point where I wanted to bust out laughing. This guy, one I looked up to for a long while, was everything I was afraid he would turn out to be. I gave him and Mateo the benefit of the doubt so many times, and Mateo proved himself to have changed. Zeke though? He just completely severed our friendship by trying to once again ruin my chances at getting the girl.

"Plus he even said that you're sleepwalking creeped him out--"

"Hey!" I pulled him by the shirt backwards, and twisted him around. I didn't need to think about my actions. It came so natural to swing my fist into his smug face as hard as I could.

He went flying backwards, running into the car behind him. Blood was running out of nose, and I think there was even a cut on his bottom lip. I wanted to keep going at him.

Zeke had been testing my patience for years, and seeing him come on to my girl and talk bullshit to her sent me over the edge. He deserved that punch to the face. I would have done it again if I had not caught Lucy's horrified expression.

"Lying dick." I yelled, shaking my hand out. "...Damn it."

Zeke had the nerve to start to laugh. "Really, Clayton? That's the best you got?"

Before my anger took over again, I did the best thing I could do. I walked away. As far as I knew, the dance that night was over for me. I needed to get home and clear my head. So I headed towards my car, with my hand throbbing in pain, and eyes low. J.K. and Lucy's other friends just came outside, probably looking for her, and I could only imagine how much of a monster they must have thought I was.

I was almost to my car when I heard the sound of footsteps behind me. I prepared myself, expecting it to be Zeke, by clenching my fist again. It ended up being the last person I thought would follow after me.

"Lucy?"

She didn't respond to me, and actually ended up storming in front of me. She wrapped around my car to the passenger side, and only then did she narrow in on me. Her green eyes were ablaze with hurt or anger. I couldn't decipher which one.

The car ride home went pretty much the same way.

I tried moving my hand to Lucy's in the car, as a sense of comfort, but she deflected my gesture by moving her hand out of reach.

Not a word was spoken between us. Not like that was some sort of surprise or anything.

To be honest, she didn't need to follow me, but she did. As far as I knew, she had planned to spend the night at J.K.'s house that evening. If she was just going to remain in that state the remaining of the night, what was the point of her coming after me?

"Aren't you supposed to be going to a friend's house tonight?" My voice shattered through the dead silence. I saw her shake a little bit. When I didn't get a response of any kind, I gazed over at her. "I'll drop you off at her house later, okay?" I got a nod that time.

The anger churning inside of me was dying down little by little as we got closer to my house. Instead of being mad, the feeling was replaced with intense disappointment. Not only did I let Lucy down and ruin her night, I let my anger get the best of me and gave Zeke exactly what he wanted. He wanted me to go crazy on him, probably to scare off the really good thing I had going with Lucy.

"I'm sorry," I finally said.

She didn't reply to me again, but that was okay. I had deserved it.

My mom was working that night, and my dad was in the city having a dinner with coworkers. So we had the whole house to ourselves, and I hated that. After all could have stayed mad at me the whole night and refuse to speak to me. If my parents were there, I was sure they would've managed a smile out of her easily.

She popped out of the car as soon as I parked. I watched as her skirt swished with the wind. Breathing out finally, I rubbed my cheeks.

Maybe if I acted like it didn't happen she would come around?

"I know you may hate me after what happened. ." Okay, maybe I couldn't pretend it didn't happen. After all, the evidence was all on my fist. "But I'll make it up to you. I promise."

We went into my house, and Lucy sat her purse on the entry table. She dug through it, and brought out her phone. She had three missed calls, each from J.K.. I didn't think when I punched Zeke about how it could affect Lucy and J.K.'s friendship. Hopefully Jacklyn Kate wasn't pissed off at me or Lucy.

"You know what we can do?" I tried to sound cheery, but it didn't seem to sway Lucy's frown. "We can binge watch all of the Harry Potter movies. How about that babe?"

It was a millisecond, but the corner of Lucy's lips curved upright.

As much as I loved my suit, it wasn't comfortable enough to lay in bed in and binge movies.

Lucy must have been thinking the same way, because the first thing she did was unclasp her necklace and place it on my dresser.

I was busy untying my tie beside her, looking at us through the mirror. Her neck was red from where the necklace was busy rubbing against her skin. She must have saw me staring, because her cheeks soon matched her neck; flushed with color.

"You really did look absolutely stunning tonight." I bit my lower lip, still fixated on her neck. I finally decided to turn towards her instead of the mirror image.

She finally smiled showing a little bit of teeth. Her green eyes flicked over to meet mine momentarily, teasing me with their beauty.

I wasn't sure what came over me, but while turning around I bent down and pressed a soft kiss to her collarbone. When I didn't get much of response from that, I moved up her neck with more. Lucy actually seemed to move her head back to give me more access, but I instantly retracted.

"Sorry. Um." I busied myself by opening my pajama drawer and pulling out some clothes for me to change into. "Did you want something to change into, too?"

Lucy stared wide eyed at me for a minute, but a sudden change in emotion caught me off guard. She nodded her head, letting out a small chuckle.

"Alright, here you go." I handed her an old t-shirt and gym shorts.

There was a twinkle in her eye I couldn't decipher. "Thanks."

Before I had a chance to leave the room and change in the closet, Lucy began to pull her dress over her shoulders, exposing her completely. Well, not exactly completely, but it was enough to make me snap my gaze somewhere else and gulp.

I had caught a glimpse of a purple bra and underwear set. I didn't think it was possible for purple to become even more of a favorite color of mine.

"Comfy," Lucy finally said, breaking the silence.

It took me a few glances to notice she decided to go without the gym shorts, and was just wearing my t-shirt.

"Yeah, I gotta go to the bathroom. I'll - uh, be back in like a minute."

Okay, maybe I took longer than a minute. I just needed time to change, and settle down before getting back out there. As much as I had Jacob in the back of my head telling me to stop whatever was going on, I really, really wanted to go farther with it. But Lucy deserved better than that, so I had to control myself. Plus both of our emotions were running high because of what happened, so neither of us are thinking clearly.

By the time I got back into my room, Lucy made herself comfortable in my bed. Although she was technically on my side of it, I let that slide.

She patted the space next to her, reaching out to hand the remote to me with a smile.

"Harry Potter time!" she squealed.

Her happiness made me over the moon. Anything to get rid of the image of her appearing so hurt at Zeke's lies.

I flicked the light off, then proceeded to get into bed with her. Even though she had plenty of space, I did notice she scooted closer to me once I was settled.

The night didn't turn out like we had planned, that was for sure. To be honest though, it could not have turned out any better. Although I've held this girl close to me for so long now, I don't think I ever felt as close to her as I did then.

We ended up watching two movies fully before we started to get tired. I could tell Lucy was tired by the way her blinking would last a second longer than usual. She would also give me a lot more lazy smiles than normal, which I found adorable.

"Did you want me to take you to J.K.'s soon?" I yawned, stretching my body out a bit.

Lucy turned flat on her stomach, cuddling up onto the pillow. It appeared like she was giving me puppy dog eyes.

"Can't I just stay here for the night? Your bed is really comfy."

It might have been a no brainer for guys like Zeke and Mateo to have girls spend the night at their houses, but I had to think about it. Mostly because I didn't want my parents finding out, and therefore having Lucy's parents find out through them and her getting in trouble.

I was mostly worried about Jacob finding out though. As cool as he was, he was a scary dude at the same time.

"Please, Clay?" She kept going with those eyes. "All we're going to do is sleep, anyways."

If her eyes weren't enough conviction, her cute voice was persuading me as well. Finally, I nodded my head.

I smirked. "Don't you think about trying anything though."

Lucy laughed softly. "Maybe next time you'll get so lucky."

She appeared to be joking, so I forced out a laugh. A part of me was hoping we would have more nights like that one.

We put the third Harry Potter movie on, but I started to drift off.

The last thing I could remember was Lucy murmuring something about being cold. Before I allowed darkness to overtake me, I fought with the covers to wrap my arm around her waist to pull her closer to me. I didn't hear a peep from her after that.

Epilogue

LUCY

I dreamed of that night. The one my parents would retell over and over again to anyone they met. About how they came across their daughter in her Barbie nightgown, eerily standing in their kitchen at a late hour. That happened almost ten years before that, and I wasn't even awake at the time to experience it, but I dreamed of it often. It felt so real every time. I could imagine my mom with her damn hockey puck, ready to smack an intruder down if she had to.

What I do remember is waking up that morning with watchful eyes on me. My parents looked so worried, and what was the first thing I blurted out?

I'm sorry for eating the last of dad's cookies. They were just so good.

I was so nervous I was going to be in trouble. Instead, I was greeted with laughter.

I used to think for the longest time that the universe punished me for finishing my dad's cookies by making me go through my sleepwalking. Let's just say I haven't had macadamia nut cookies since that day.

The sun was what woke me up.

It began to stream through the window, burning my eyes as I attempted to squint them open. It took me a few moments to process where I was, but it didn't take that long. After all, there was arm still wrapped securely around me.

At first, my heart warmed up at the idea of Clayton holding on to me throughout the whole night, but then it nearly leaped out of my chest.

Was I still in the same position as when we had fallen asleep last night?

There was a chance I had gotten up overnight and Clayton laid me back down. I tried keeping the happiness bubbling inside me down, in case of that scenario. I didn't need to disappointment myself.

However it was no use. I looked up towards Clayton and his sleeping face was more precious than anything. I scanned over him.

When I was that fourteen year old girl seeing a guy like Clayton Hugh enter her class, my crush was almost instant. There was always something about him that caught my eye - my heart, and no matter how hard I tried, it would never shake. My friends poked fun at me for my crush, like any friends of course. They told me he was a douchebag like all of the other jock guys at our school. At first I believed that because, well, it was true.

I never blamed Clayton for being that way though. He was handsome, foreign, and great at athletics. Guys like him were destined for being a lady's man and being every guy's best friend. For the longest time I let myself have a crush from afar and never approach him because of that.

Clayton's breathing was steady and light. The sunlight was casting over his face, almost highlighting his freckles.

Like I had thought before, there was always that chance he had put be back in the bed last night. I knew he hadn't though.

I knew, deep down, that sleeping next to him may very well be my remedy.

It made complete sense to me. He made me feel safe and secure at any point we were together. Although I have tried sleeping with other people I cared about, I had never slept soundly through the whole night. Clayton and I's connection went beyond that of my friends and family. It was something I had never experienced before.

I relished in whatever it was I was feeling, until Clayton began to stir. He straightened out the arm laying across my back, and eventually I saw those blue-green eyes poking out into the day. He eventually turned around to be on his back, and stretched his body out.

"Good morning," I whispered at first, testing if he was actually awake yet.

When I received an eyes closed turn of the face towards me, I took that as he was awake. "Hi."

I couldn't help but giggle at his groggy, deep voice.

"God, what time is it?" He rubbed at his eyes.

I sat up, peering at his alarm clock. "Close to twelve-thirty."

Reaching over to my phone, I checked my notifications to find texts from J.K. There was six of them, and all of them were forms of apologizing for Zeke's douchebaggery and how she wanted nothing to do with him anymore. She apparently snuck in her own damage on him last night by kicking him right in the eggplant emoji. Whatever that meant.

Smirking to myself, I pulled the covers off me and stood up. And to think, the night previous I was scared our friendship would be ruined over something like that. I should've known she wouldn't allow bullshit in her life. Especially one that tried to sabotage a friend's relationship with someone.

Clayton eventually followed suit and got out of bed. He left his room to see if either of his parents were home, and he came and told me just his mom was, but she was sound asleep.

Being the gentleman he was, he went to his car and brought my bag in that had spare clothes in it. I wasn't going to tell Clayton this, but that was the main reason why I followed after him after he had punched Zeke. Then it turned into me wanting to make sure he was alright, even though I was pretty high in emotion at the beginning.

"So did you want to take me home soon?" I asked Clayton, although I was hoping the answer would be a straight up no.

Thankfully, that was what I got. "I was actually hoping we could go to a few places today."

I pursed my lips. "Interesting. Like what places?"

"Well. . I was thinking we could start the day off with some milkshakes?"

The smile on my face had to of been blinding.

After all, the day was starting off amazingly. I woke up in the same position I fell asleep in, got to wake up next to a gorgeous specimen, and now milkshakes? I was over-the-moon.

We settled at our usual table at Shakers, earning a few hello's from the staff.

Effie, the cashier, actually came up to our table and commented on how I looked last night.

"You looked so pretty last night, Lucy." She beamed. Then, her smile suddenly lightened. "I'm sorry to hear about what happened with you guys and Zeke though. He's telling people Clayton started things, but I know that's a lie."

Clayton rolled his eyes and finished his sip of his milkshake. "That guy doesn't know when to quit."

Effie quickly apologized, like her usual self, in case she caused Clayton any discomfort by mentioning him. After about another ten apologizes later from her, she left us to attend to another customer.

"I know we didn't talk about it last night," I began. "But I wanted you to know I'm sorry for believing what Zeke was saying for a split second. I was just taken off guard and--"

Clayton instantly started to shake his head. "No. No way, don't apologize. You have nothing to apologize for. If anything, I should have apologized and explained myself to you last night." He sighed. "I never thought I'd resort to violence like that. I hope you know that's not me."

I proceeded to take a long sip of my milkshake. I could feel his eyes on me, analysing. Finally, I said, "it's okay. Zeke is a moron."

Our eyes met momentarily. I could tell he was still battling with his own demons about yesterday, and I had wished he wouldn't. He was the nicest guy I knew, but even the nicest have their breaking point. To be honest, if Clayton hadn't showed up, I probably would have punched Zeke in the face myself.

It's like their whole friendship was Zeke's way of making sure Clayton never blossomed into something more than a clone of him.

"On a lighter note, after this we're gonna go to the music shop."

My brows perked up. "Really?"

Clayton nodded, finally smiling. "Yep. I haven't been there for so long, and figured a fellow rock enthusiast like yourself would like to attend with me."

The last time I had went to The Tunes was that time Clayton came up to me randomly and I made a fool out of myself. That felt like absolute ages ago.

"Uh, sure. That sounds cool."

We continued on talking about random things and drinking our milk shakes, but once we finished, we headed towards the music shop. It was a beautiful day out, not too hot or too cold. As we strolled to the other side of the shopping center though, I couldn't help but notice he was glancing at his phone a lot.

I chose to shrug it off. It wasn't any of my business anyways.

We stayed at the music shop for a long time. Way longer than I had ever been there before, too. Clayton and I had always shared our love for T.V. shows together, since we had just about binged every great series on Netflix, but we hadn't touched music yet together. Which is kind of ironic, sense we first actually crossed paths there.

He showed me a lot of rock and roll artists, some from America, but most international. I would show him some of my favorite artists ranging from R&B to bubblegum pop, and we were having a good time overall with each other.

We might have stayed there a little longer if Clayton didn't hear my stomach growl.

"Hungry?"

Nodding, I grabbed my stomach dramatically.

"Yeah. I probably should go home soon, my mom will have dinner made soon."

Clayton peered down at his phone once again, this time for a good second, then paid his attention back to me. He shook his head.

"I called your dad if it was okay we hung out the rest of the day together while you went to the restroom, and he said it was fine. If he asks though, just say I picked you up from J.K.'s house right about now." He scratched the back of his neck. "I hate lying, but, yeah.."

I didn't really have much to say to that. I was mostly hungry and trying to figure out where I was going to get that food. If I wasn't going home for dinner, then we needed to get to the nearest restaurant as soon as possible.

"How about that restaurant we went to after the movies a few weeks ago?"

My stomach growled at the thought of Mexican food.

"I guess I'll be taking that as a yes?" He chuckled.

It was safe to say I scarfed down my food as quick as possible. I probably could have continued munching on the endless chips and salsa, but Clayton started to rush me. He said we had another stop somewhere, and then he would take me back home.

"Where are we going now?" I questioned.

Clayton smirked over at me. "You'll see."

The way he was acting was starting to make me suspicious. He seemed all too knowing about everything we were doing. There was no way all of these places were just randomly popping in his mind to go.

"Can I get a hint at least?" I squeezed his hand a little tighter. I noticed we were walking back towards his car.

Smiling, he nods. "Yeah, sure. It's one of my favorite places."

He laughed because of my scrunched up face.

"That could be so many places, Clay!"

"Then guess what, you'll have to wait see, now won't you?" He was still defiant, and it was driving me nuts.

He let my hand go to unlock his car, and away we went. I paid extra attention to the route we were taking, still spewing out guesses after guesses. All I would get in return was an amused expression.

It felt like ages we were stuck in that car. If I didn't know better, I thought we were going in circles. I could have sworn we had passed the same church three times. I let it slide however, and tried my best to be patient.

"The baseball field?"

I narrowed in on the field as it came into view. When Clayton didn't spew out a teasing maybe, I knew that was the place we were going to. Especially when I caught a glimpse of a group of people walking towards the parking lot, about to leave.

Clayton honked his horn, prompting hoots and hollers from my brother, Jacklyn Kate, Mateo, and Abby. Jacob was waving erratically, causing a laugh to escape me.

"What's going on, Clay?" I placed my hand on his forearm, hoping he would give me an answer at least this once.

Unsurprisingly, I got no response in return.

As he parked the car, I noticed the group going into Jacob's truck.

They were leaving already? We had just gotten there, and I couldn't imagine what two people could be doing at a baseball field. I was starting to think we were gonna play a scrimmage game possibly, but that idea flew out the window as I watched them pull out to leave.

"Remember what we talked about, Clayton!" Jacob stuck his head out of the back window. He was pointing towards Clayton. "Take care of my sister."

We got out of his car, and since it was starting to get dark, it was beginning to get a little chilly. I hadn't expected to be outside today, so I didn't bring a jacket with me. Clayton didn't miss a beat though, grabbing one conveniently in his trunk.

"Okay, so what are we doing here?" I hugged myself, enjoying wearing his jacket a little too much.

Clayton gestured for me to follow him. "Come on. You'll see right over here."

As we walked closer to the baseball field, I noticed there were twinkly lights set up around the dugouts and metal fences. They were a bright white; lighting the field ever so slightly with the help of the moonlight. I could begin to make out the soft playing of music, the slow kind that couples would slow dance to. It left me baffled, yet dazzled at the same time.

"What..." I couldn't help but hang my mouth open.

I turned my head, meeting the brightest of smiles. He looked all too knowing and proud at the field he practiced so hard at.

"I know this isn't like the dance last night. . but I was wanting to make it up to you." He jogged away from me towards a speaker near the home plate. He turned a nozzle to make the music louder. "You've been looking forward to the dance way too long, and I ruined that for you."

I was too busy looking around at the lights to notice he had walked back beside me. His arm brushed mine, making me jump a little.

I was still processing what exactly was going on. The whole day I had seen him on his phone, but now it made sense. He was planning this alongside our friends.

"You did all of this for me?" My heart was thudding in my chest. His infinite smile was only making it harder.

Clayton reached out and grabbed my hand, his thumb softly sliding back and forth on my skin. "Of course."

"But. ." My eyes moved around the dancing lights. "Why?"

That was when he took my other hand, too. He squeezed them both softly, while his smile softened too. He opened his mouth to speak once, but stopped.

"Did you wanna dance?" He asked a few moments later, randomly. He had a sheepish grin. "I actually really like this song."

It was Ed Sheeran's Thinking Out Loud. That was one of my favorite songs, and Clayton knew this, too.

He took my smile as a yes, and moved my hands to go around his neck. His moved around my waist, his fingertips digging into my hips a little too hard. I could tell he was nervous about something, but I wasn't sure about what just yet.

We swayed back and forth together, my head finding a place to lay on his chest. I could hear his erratic heartbeat, and it ironically was more beautiful to me than the song. It soothed my own down, and eventually my eyes closed shut.

The song ended soon after, but we stayed put for a couple songs after that.

Then, finally, Clayton said, "and to answer your question. . ." He breathed out before continuing. "I did this because I really, really like you, Lucy." The minute the words came off his tongue I my gaze snapped to his. He was turning a bright red. His eyes moved towards the ground, then he gulped. "I've been crazy about you for a while now. It just, uh, took me way too long to tell you."

In my head the past couple of years, I came up with so many imaginary scenarios Clayton Hugh would confess his feelings for me. One was in a dream where he came knocking at my door (shirtless, for whatever reason), and confessed it was love at first sight with me. Another was much more realistic, where he had asked me to our senior prom and we won prom king and queen. Then there was the time we would partner up on a project, and he would be overcome with his adoration for me that he just kissed out of the blue.

This, though, was better than anything I could have imagined though.

It was real, happening, and I just did the first thing that came to mind.

I stood up on my tiptoes, staring back at him for a few moments. His eyes flicked between both of mine, and his nose was slightly scrunched up. I could tell he was about to say something else, maybe about why I was right there, but I pulled his head forward before he could.

My lips met his in an instant.

For a few seconds, it didn't even feel like our lips were connected. I had went absolutely numb from my lips all the way to the toes

I was standing on, but then he finally kissed me back. Only then did my lips begin to tingle as they were engulfed by soft, tentative kisses. His mouth was so sweet; everything I knew they would be and more. He pulled me closer to him, making me almost fall into him clumsily. I think he smiled through the kiss because of that, but I wasn't so sure. All I knew was that I could have kept kissing him for hours, but he was the one who pulled back.

He was flushed with color on his cheeks and lips as we moved apart, and his eyes looked to be a in a daze. I couldn't help but stare at his mouth, wanting nothing more to kiss him again.

"Wow.. uh." Clayton chuckled awkwardly. "I was starting to think that would never happen."

I went back and pressed another kiss to his lips. Then I smiled at him, giggling a bit. "Me either."

The rest of our little dance went a lot like that. We continued slow dancing, kissing from time to time, and confessing so many things.

"You really wished to have me notice you as your birthday wish?" Clayton didn't even bother to hide his smirk.

I scoffed. "What? Don't blame a girl for wanting to get her crush's attention."

Clayton shrugged a little. "Well, that was a waste of a wish. That's all I'm saying."

"How was I supposed to know you had some sort of not-so-but-kind-of crush on me from afar?" I blasted back at him, laughing.

"Touché, love. Touché." He laughed along with me. I could feel his chest vibrate on my face as we continued slow dancing. "Hey, Lucy. . I actually meant to ask you something this morning."

Clayton pressed on my cheek with his hand, gesturing to look up at him. He placed a loose hair behind my ear and I thought for a moment he was going to kiss me again, but sadly he didn't.

"How did you sleep last night?"

I smiled at his question.

The past couple of months forming a friendship with Clayton through trying to find a way to stop my bizarre sleepwalking has been an interesting one for sure. I went through a disgusting green diet, yoga classes to relieve stress, and several other ideas that ultimately failed.

Sleepwalking had always seemed like a curse to me, but now I was thankful for it. After all, it led me right to Clayton Hugh, my remedy. It may have been a tough road, but in that moment, dancing with Clayton, I felt like everything was going to be okay. There may be more obstacles in my future, sure, but I could feel deep down that sleepwalking wouldn't be as much of an issue anymore.

"Honestly?"

Clayton nodded me on.

"Better than I have in a long, long time."

www.ingramcontent.com/pod-product-compliance
Lightning Source LLC
Chambersburg PA
CBHW070936190726
48292CB00004B/1197